ETA CARINAE

Brian d'Eon

Home Star Press

ALSO BY BRIAN D'EON

Big Ledge: The Triumphs and Tribulations
of Robert E. Sproule

Loose Ends

The Draper Catalogue

Echoes: What if the Stones Could Speak?

Letters to Icarus

Lunatics

HOME STAR PRESS
6-1004 Eighth St.
Nelson, BC V1L 3B3

ISBN

978-1-7753872-5-1 (eBook)
978-1-7753872-4-4 (Paperback)
978-1-7753872-6-8 (Audiobook)

1. FICTION

Front Cover: Uluru
Unless otherwise noted, all photos are from the author's personal collection.

for my best mate, J.

We are all visitors to this time.
This place we are just passing through.
Our purpose here is to observe.
To learn. To grow. To love.
And then we return home.

AUSTRALIAN ABORIGINAL PROVERB

CHAPTER ONE

The Australian Outback: April 1843

It had always been said that Star Dancer did not need to travel as other men. He knew the stars so well that, in his dreaming, he could hop from point to point as a man might step on the backs of turtles in a running stream.

But out of courtesy to his tribe, for the time being, his feet remained earth-bound.

The Southern Milky Way

Queensland Coast: April 2015

Not far from the Minister for Parks and Aboriginal Affairs, two young women lay topless on lounge chairs, enjoying the late morning sun. They were up from Melbourne where, by this time of the year, summer—even the stretched-out summer of recent memory—was clearly over, and the cool rains had begun. The smiles on their faces, the content beaming from the corners of their closed eyes, all spoke of how good it was that they were here but their colleagues were down south.

Palm fronds swayed in the gentle breeze. Little green leaf-cutter ants worked meticulously in the foliage above. A great swarm of rainbow lorikeets flew past—their wing flaps an audible *whoosh* as they raced madly towards succulent gum blossoms.

The *whoosh* was the sound of work back home. It was the footsteps in the hall, the beepers, the fax machines, the speeches in parliament, the interviews with the Press. They were all now a *whoosh* far away, a breeze almost inaudible, and the Minister from Canberra found that his eyelids too were closing, though not without protest, for he saw those youthful bosoms vividly in his mind's eye and imagined he and they floating peacefully somewhere, bobbing up and down in a tepid sea.

The Minister's eyes had just closed when he heard a cry. "Hey, watch it!" It was one of the refugees from Melbourne. She had been splashed by the kick turn of a ten-year-old Olympic-hopeful, busy doing laps in the pool.

Good on yer, thought the Minister, till he saw the Melbourner grab a towel and cover herself up. They *were* planning to go in for a swim themselves, weren't they? But, on reflection, the Minister realized they wouldn't. In fact, a moment later, a large cloud covered the sun and that was enough. Both women pulled on jumpers, and began to talk about where to go for lunch.

Lunch—of all things—it was no concern of his.

The magazine the Minister had been holding began to slip from his grasp, sheltered from its fall for a moment by his ample abdomen but inexorably sliding down —along the side of his shorts, off the edge of the lounge, and down to the hard concrete of poolside. A kookaburra stared at the sleeping Minister, mesmerized by the up and down movement of his stomach, wondering, if somewhere in that mass of flesh, there might be a juicy witchity grub.

"What? What is it? I'm on *holiday*!" The Minister's voice was unusually loud and seemed to echo in some great hall. Where was he? But the god-damn beeping persisted. Would they never leave him alone? And then a great drop of rain landed on his stomach. "Damn!" the Minister yelled. He opened an eye. "It's not supposed to rain up here!" Three more drops of rain fell, one a direct hit on his navel. "Bloody hell! Won't they ever leave me alone!"

Patrick had resisted bringing the mobile, and they had assured him they would only call in the event of an emergency, but Patrick knew how it would turn out. He knew. He held the phone in his palm and momentarily thought of chucking it into the bush but settled, instead, on a rant. "Yes! What is it?" He was the only one at poolside now. The rain was falling in great drops and he held the magazine over his head. A picture of rugby star, Val Bendigo, received the worst of it, his thick curly hair already turned to mush. "This better be good!"

On the other end of the line was the Minister's personal secretary. She was used to his abuse; she spoke calmly, removed herself to another world, and with admirable professionalism delivered the message.

"What? They're doing what? What the hell for? Oh bloody hell. Bloody, bloody hell. And I suppose they want me to go down there? Look, did you tell the PM? Did you tell him this is the first holiday I've—what? Jesus! All right. All right. Well, what's Jim's number then? Right. Right. Good on yer, Sharon. Right."

The Minister disconnected. "Well I'll just send Jim then. Hell, he's an Abo, isn't he? Maybe at last he'll do something to earn his keep! You better bloody well be home, Jim boy." The Minister suddenly realized he had been talking out loud to himself for a good half-minute, at least. What the hell? Why should he care?

Pissed off that he'd never learned the speed dial thing, the Minister punched the numbers on the phone with renewed ferocity, more determined than ever to guard his holiday from any further sabotage.

James Cook was twenty-nine. Although he in no way resembled his famous naval namesake, he had still done well for himself. He was senior advisor to the Minister for Parks and Aboriginal Affairs, and it was made known to him that, if he didn't rock the boat too much, if he played his cards *right,* he might very well find himself sitting in parliament one day. As it was, the government was very proud to be able to point to Jim and say, "You see, this is just one small indication of our government's commitment to equality of opportunity for all Australia's people."   Most days, it was all a little much. Jim was no fool. If his ethnic background could be used to boost his career opportunities, so be it, but he had no interest in being a spokesperson for his "people". He really never thought of them as *his* people at all. Well, at least no more than he thought of the North Melbourne Kangaroos as *his* rugby team. It was an accident of birth, at best, of residency, more likely. Hell, he didn't even look aboriginal particularly. His hair had a bit of a curl, and you certainly couldn't call him light-skinned, but he might easily pass for a Mediterranean. At Uni, he sometimes proclaimed that his ancestry was Spanish and most people believed him. His grandmother was from Ireland, so who knows, it might have been something less than an unabashed lie. The sun had been up just half an hour as James's plane made its final descent into Prosperine. A monotony of stunted eucalyptus forest lay beneath as far as one could see. Not even the plane's shadow brought relief to the parched scene. It was strange how the trees were neatly spaced from each other, antisocial, almost as if they had been planted that way, but who would make a plantation of gum trees?

Jeez, thought James, it was hard to believe anyone actually *chose* to live here. If the land had any wealth in it, it wasn't obvious to the eye. And this was only the fringe. To the west and the north and south, lay land even more barren—treeless, red, vast, burning with silence. But he wouldn't have to deal with that today.

"Jimmy! Jimmy boy! Over here!"

He hadn't expected to be met by the Minister, and was momentarily shocked to see him dressed so informally. My God, thought James, why do so many white fellas have ugly knees?

"You'll have to get rid of that suit and tie, mate. Come on, we've got to hurry. Come on, get in." It was only 7:30 in the morning, but already the Minister was sweating profusely.

"But my luggage—"

"Na, na, forget about that, we'll get it later. You got a cozzie?"

"In my carry-on." James patted the bag slung round his shoulder. He had lost airport luggage too many times.

"Well that's right, then, come on, we've got to be in Shute Harbour by 9:00."

Perhaps the Minister thought there was something ecclesiastical about his title. At any rate, Patrick Mahoney, the Minister for Parks and Aboriginal Affairs, drove like a nun, seeming to believe he was exempt from ordinary physical laws. He drove too fast, accelerated at the most unlikely times, and seemed to feel that the application of brakes implied an essential lack of faith. James stared at the Minister and imagined what he would look like in a full habit.

"What are you staring at Jim boy?"

"What?"

The Minister had formed a career around the principle of looking people *squarely in the eye.*

"Nothing, Minister, nothing. I was just daydreaming. Watch out, sir. There's a—"

"I see it, Jimmy boy, no worries." They swerved around the koala bear who seemed to have run out of steam right in the middle of the bitumen. James looked back after they had driven by—it showed no signs of continuing its journey and James wondered what would become of it.

"You know people say we have a koala problem, but there's no koala problem. There's millions of those little buggers all over the place. My sister has a whole family of them living under her house in Brisbane. They're everywhere. It's all you can do to keep from stepping on them. I saw this bloke on the telly the other night saying how they're all stressed out from living in the proximity of humans. Well, join the club, I say! Stressed out! I guess *we're* a little stressed out having to dodge 'round them on the roadways every day and climbing up telephone poles to help the stupid little buggers find their way home!"

"I reckon," James replied.

There was a pause. The Minister seemed to be thinking. This wasn't something James had observed often. "So when did you get that thing in your ear?"

"What?"

"How long have you had that …?"

"Earring?"

Earring, right."

"I don't know, Minister, a couple of years, I guess."

"A couple of years?" The Minister was surprised. "Funny—this is the first time I ever noticed—it doesn't have any special …?"

"It's just an earring, sir. A fashion statement."

"There you go then. I always knew you were a sensible bloke."

"Thank you, sir."

"Now don't start calling me, sir, for Christ's sake—I'm not some bloody pommy Lord or something."

"No sir."

"Right, then. I suppose you've been wondering where we're going. Well, you're in luck, my boy, because today I'm taking us out to the Reef—have you ever been to the GBR before, Jim?"

"Well actually, sir—what *should* I call you then, if not—"

"Minister's all right. Or you can even call me Pat. There's no reason we shouldn't be on a first name basis, is there?"

"Pat? You're sure? Okay. Well, no, Pat … I never have been to the Reef."

"Well, that makes two of us! Never had the time. But you've got to *make* time for things, don't you Jim boy! You don't live forever, do you?"

"No sir—Pat."

They drove mostly in silence for the next twenty minutes. James had serious doubts they would be in Shute Harbour by 9:00 but the Minister seemed unperturbed.

"I mean there's no reason to cut my holiday short just because this has come up, is there? A man is entitled to his holiday time, no matter who he is— am I right? I mean it's in our bloody constitution, isn't it? Or it should be."

"It only seems fair."

"I planned to see the Reef today, and so that's what I'm going to do. I mean I'd already reserved the bloody tickets, hadn't I?"

"There's no reason you can't brief me on the ferry."

"Exactly. Kill two birds with one stone. Anyway, I reckon you've probably always wanted to the see the Reef. I mean it's something every Aussie has to do, isn't it?"

"I suppose."

"To my way of thinking, there's the Sydney Opera House, the Melbourne Cricket Ground, Ayer's Rock and the Reef—you can't really call yourself an Australian if you haven't visited at least them, right?"

"Well, I—"

"Oh yes, and the Twelve Apostles! But I suspect you've been there heaps of times, being a Melbourne boy and all."

"Well actually, Pat—"

"And tomorrow we're going to send you to the Rock, so that should do it for you, eh, Jim boy? You'll become an official Australian!"

The Minister's monologue was interrupted by the sound of their ferry blowing its whistle. "No worries, Jim." The Minister began to blow his own car horn furiously as he swerved into the parking lot. He screeched to a halt in a spot marked "Reserved" and quickly opened the door for Jim. "So, out you go, Jim! Tell them they can't leave without the Minister! Go on, go on!"

Ten minutes behind schedule, a disgruntled ferry captain eased his vessel out of port. It glided effortlessly on its two pontoons, soon sliding into the open water and into sight of Daydream Island. A second ferry, from a rival company, pulled up only fifty metres to the starboard. Country music played from the ship's loudspeakers and Jim could see passengers applying sunscreen to their incredibly pale arms and legs. James waved. The albinos waved back.

"Here, Jim, you better take one of these." The Minister handed his assistant two little white pills.

"What are they?"

"Once we get out into the open water, it gets a little rough. Go on, take one."

James swallowed. "What about you, Minister?"

"Hey, not too loud, Jimmy boy! I don't want any special treatment."

"Oh," James exclaimed in genuine surprise, "sorry."

"I don't need the pills, Jimmy. My family comes from a long line of seafarers— we're used to the open sea. Hey, but look who I'm talking to. *James Cook!*"

James smiled and excused himself to search for some crisps.

The ferry passed by numerous sailing boats of all sizes and even a few kayaks. Mariners of every description seemed to be out in the passage, having in common with each other at least the serious determination to *take it easy.* From where James stood, it was a convincing illusion, and he sighed, trying to imagine himself lounging on a yacht or even on a small sailboat.

As they headed east, the forests of Whitsunday Island loomed ever larger on the starboard. They were heading for the narrow passage between Whitsunday and Hook Island, and then it would be a straight run through open water till they arrived at the Reef. When James returned from the canteen, he found the Minister slouched in a seat directly in front of the big screen TV. His mouth was open and he was gently snoring. James wondered what would happen if he popped in a crisp.

"The Great Barrier Reef is the greatest living artifact on the planet Earth." The monitor was showing pictures of the reef and its many and varied inhabitants. James had never really stopped to consider that there might exist an entire other world beneath the water, beneath his feet at this very moment, moreover a world totally different and totally independent of him. He was starting to get very interested.

"So, you're back? You weren't up-chucking over the railing, were you?"

"I feel fine, Minister." The female voice doing the commentary was very pleasant, almost hypnotic, but James thought he heard a hint of a New Zealand accent, maybe even Maori. He hoped against hope that they might show a picture of the commentator. "You should see this, Minister. It's fascinating."

"A lot of fish, I know."

"Well, not just fish, look, they've got tortoises down there—no turtles—actually, I'm not sure what the difference—God, look at that! Look at the size of it! What do they call that fish?" The Maori commentator obliged by informing them they were looking at a Giant Wrasse. "*Giant*, I'll say!"

"So, Jimmy boy, shall we get down to work?"

"Right, sir—Pat." James threw his plastic wrapper in the bin and quickly took a pad and pen out of his bag.

"No laptop?"

"Broken, sir."

Pat grunted. "Broken? Hmph ... The whole bloody Ministry's broken."

"So, what's this all about, sir? They hardly told me anything over the phone."

"No, they wouldn't, those bastards. They like to make it as cloak-and-dagger as possible. Well, here's what it is then: we've got a problem up at Ayer's Rock."

"Uluru?"

"Right.... Well, you just knew it was going to happen sometime, didn't you? I mean it's all very well and fine to hand the rock back to the Abos—sorry, Jimmy, I forget sometimes—aboriginals—" He put a hand on James's shoulder.

"No worries, Minister."

"Well, so we hand it back to them, give them joint jurisdiction over the place, make the whole thing into a world-class park, but you just knew one day they were going to ask for it back."

"I don't follow, Minister."

"Well, it's just like I said. They want the Rock back. They say it belongs to them, and they want us to clear out."

"What do you mean?"

"It's not hard to understand, mate. They want us to clear out. The Park Rangers, the hotel staff, even the airport people—they want anybody with white skin to take a hike."

"Permanently?"

"Well, how the hell should I know? That's one of the reasons, I'm sending you there, to find out what's going on."

"You want *me* to go, sir?"

"Yes. I've booked you on a flight tomorrow: Proserpine—Brisbane—Alice Springs."

"But why me, sir?"

"Well, they're not going to tell *me* what they're really thinking, are they? But *you,* one of their own—"

"But Minister, I'm from Melbourne, they're from the Territory. I don't even speak—"

"I've every confidence in you, my boy. I want you to get as friendly with them as you can—well, within limits, of course. I don't want you to go feral on me or anything!"

"Minister, I —"

"Just kidding, Jimmy boy! You can take a joke, can't you?"

"Minister, maybe I'm just a little thick, but I still don't understand exactly what you want me to—"

"Just get to know them, Jimmy. Keep your ears and eyes open. Find out what's really going on. Is this another Mabo thing or what? I mean, in terms of revenue we simply can't give up the park, you know that."

"It doesn't seem very feasible."

"Do you realize how many people fly into the Rock every year?"

James couldn't tell if this was rhetorical question or not, so he spoke slowly, "I don't have the exact figure."

"Hundreds of thousands. From all over the world, Jimmy. From Japan. From Germany. From America. Geez, we even get Australians coming there. It's a world-class tourist attraction and it brings in millions to the Territory, millions."

"They can't want to shut it down permanently."

"I don't know what they want. That's what you're going there to find out. And don't take too long about it. God knows how much money we've lost already. They've blockaded the airport and the only way the tourists can get out is by bus to bloody Alice or bloody Adelaide, for God's sake."

"It's serious then?"

"You think I'd be interrupting my holiday if wasn't serious, mate?"

The ferry's slowing motors and the captain's voice brought the briefing to an effective end. "Ladies and gentleman, in a few minutes we'll be tying up at the Seaquest pontoon, and you'll be free to have a close-up look at the world famous Outer Reef. The weather today looks quite good; the wind is light, and skies should remain mostly sunny. The present water temperature is 22° C. We encourage all of you to get into the water and visit the Reef's many wonders. However, for those of you unable to do that, we have at our disposal a submarine especially designed for touring the site. However you decide to spend your time, have a great day, and we'll see you in a couple of hours.

"Ladies, please be advised that some species of reef fish are particularly attracted to bright dangly jewellery which, as a rule, you should not wear into the water."

Most people were already out on the deck, many with their masks in place and some adjusting their flippers.

The sight of all these pale creatures readying themselves to leap into the open ocean made James's eyes pop wide open. "So, are you going in, Minister?"

"Come on, I'll show you where you can hire a wetsuit."

"I can't swim, Minister."

"You don't have to swim. You just have to float. They have these floaties you can use. Come on."

"I don't know, Minister. Maybe the submarine—"

"Ah come on, Jimmy, have a go. You don't want to go in a bloody yellow submarine. Men don't go in submarines. Come on, let's get you some flippers."

James had one last card to play. "It's not something aboriginals do, sir."

Patrick Mahoney paused in mid-step, and then responded as he always did when unsure of himself, with a great belly-laugh. "Ah, you kill me, Jimmy, you really do!"

CHAPTER TWO

Outside the jet's window, James saw through bleary eyes that it was all true: the country was red, red and barren, with only salt basins and pale desiccated river beds for relief. The shadow of a solitary cloud momentarily confused the scene, its purple darkness suggesting a lake, but there was no lake.

"Can I get you something to drink, sir?"

The stewardess was like James's grandmother, hair as red as the rusted rock. She might have done well in a Nicole Kidman look-alike contest.

"What have you got?"

"Beer, fizzie, juice."

"Have you got something with passion fruit in it?"

The stewardess smiled, reached for the juice container, then poured. "Going home for a visit?"

"No, no, I'm from Melbourne. I'm going to Alice on business."

"I see." The stewardess handed him his drink.

"So, what's Alice like then?"

"Very hot."

"Oh well, won't be much of a place for a Melbourner, then, will it?"

The stewardess smiled, ignored the question: "We should be arriving in just under an hour, sir."

"Time for a little more shut-eye then. Thanks."

"No worries, sir."

The drone and gentle vibration of the plane was soothing, harking back to the days when James would ride in the back of the wagon with his mother, pulled by Uncle Mandy's ancient horse. Travelling ever so slowly up, up, higher into the hills toward mighty Mt. Bongon, a vision which gradually and strangely changed into images of parrot fish, tangs, anemones, giant wrasses, all swimming in lazy circles around James's submerged and puzzled face. "But I'm from Melbourne," James kept explaining, but the fish didn't seem to care.

And then more dreams, an endless stream of bizarre images and jumbled recollections, finally ending with a sequence that was remarkable for its vividness and which didn't seem to include him at all:

An old man woke suddenly from under a large tree. The oppressive heat of midday had eased, and there was the smell of honey in the air. The old man stretched his limbs, rose, spat, and called out to his family in a language James didn't recognize.

Long shadows raced across the plain. Uluru glowed like a hot ember, deep red, then brown, consuming itself, finally visible only in the eyes of sliding serpents.

James could see that soon nothing would darken the plain as well as Uluru. It would be a darkness within the darkness, a place where no stars shone. Now, in the last moments of twilight, it stood before the old man like a giant stringed gourd dropped from the sky.

From all directions, dingoes began to howl, confused by the silhouettes of people ruffling the western sky. The cicadas too sang out, roaring in their hundreds of thousands—the sound stars would make if they had voices. A dozen slender men lined up in single file behind the old man. Snakelike they began to weave their way between the clumps of spinifex, faintly chanting as they moved.

Hours later, one simple thought ricocheted in James's head: thank God for air-conditioning. He was sitting in the middle of a nearly empty bus, barrelling down the middle of an arrow-straight road in the middle of nowhere. Barrelling, mind you. As if with a purpose. James was innately suspicious of anyone or anything which seemed to have a "purpose".

The remainder of the passenger manifest consisted of one German couple, two young men from Finland, and a young woman whom James guessed must be from Sydney. James pulled back his curtain and looked briefly out his window. There it was: the outback, beyond the black stump, Nothingland. James let escape a long and luxurious sigh as he settled back in his seat, hoping, this time, his sleep would be free of dreaming.

Which it seemed to be until, sometime later, it was interrupted by a voice:

"Ladies and gentlemen, if you look out on your right, you'll see an example of the goanna, Australia's largest lizard. Some individuals can grow to over two metres in size. Although they may look ferocious, they can really do you little harm." The German was adjusting his camera, switching to the continuous shoot mode, presumably. After he'd taken his several dozen shots, the driver put the bus back in gear and slowly pulled away.

"We should be arriving in Uluru in about thirty minutes, ladies and gentlemen. As you know, we are experiencing certain labour disputes at the moment so there may some trouble finding accommodation. Our bus continues on to Adelaide, so if worse comes to worst, you can join me for that part of the run in about ... six hours from now."

The countryside was greener than James had expected: semi-desert, not desert proper. There were even trees of a sort—desert oaks—and everywhere the land was spotted with bushes, even flowers—in places huge mats of violet parakelya which seemed to sprout directly from the red sand. It had rained last week, the driver explained, and everything had been transformed.
"So," said the woman from Sydney, "what do you think?"

She had to be a journalist. Pushy. Probably had a micro-tape recorder hidden on her.

"Come on, you must know *something*. Why would you be out here if you didn't know something?" The journalist stuck out her hand. "The name's Pam."

After rubbing his eyes, James was finally able to focus—pleasant face to look at. "Pleased to meet you, Pamela. I'm James."

"Pam."

"Pam, it is."

"So, James … " She leaned closer as if to tell a secret. "What do you think they're planning?"

"Really, Pam, you know just as much about it as I do.”

Clearly Pam didn't believe him but, undeterred, continued. "Are there any decent places to eat in Uluru, do you think?"

James shrugged. "It's my first time."

Pam spat out what appeared to be the shell of a sunflower seed. "What about the others? What do you think *they*'re up to?"

"Just tourists, as far as I can see."

"*Nobody's* ever *just* a tourist."

"No?"

Pam shook her head, then returned to her seat, there opening a fresh bag of sunflower seeds, demonstrating to all that *she*, at least, knew how to be content with little.

"Here we are, ladies and gentlemen, the Uluru Hilton." A rush of hot dry air entered the bus as the door opened. "I'm afraid the best you'll manage is a bit of do-it-yourself. The Hostel's still open— well, sort of—you'll mostly have to fend for yourself. The true-blue Aussie way, eh?"

Uluru

The great red monolith defied normal expectations. It was too large, too red. It was easier to imagine it as a cardboard cut-out, a Hollywood backdrop, rather than something real, looming, breaking through a surface that was meant to be flat and endless.

"This is Ayer's Rock?" one of the Finns asked, aiming his camcorder as he spoke.

"That's it," James answered.

"And this?" The Finn pointed in the opposite direction.

My God, how did I miss that? Had he been asleep when they drove by? "That must be Kata Djuta."

The Finn looked confused. This did not sound English. "Kata? Kata?"

"The Olgas," Pam explained.

"Yes, that's what the Europeans call them. But the aboriginals call them *Kata Djuta.*" Pam smirked as she watched James set the record straight.

The Olgas. It was a name the Finns recognized: "The Olgas, yes!

They are beautiful. How far away?"

James shrugged. "I don't know, ten, fifteen kilometres, maybe more."

"Then we can walk, yes?" said the Finn, the Nordic excitement almost splitting the seams of his shorts.

"I don't think you want to do that, mate. At any rate, not at this hour. Come on, let's go see if we can find a room."

It was happening again. It often happened and James could never understand why. Somehow he had been thrust into a position of leadership. It couldn't be his decisiveness. No one had ever accused him of that. Maybe it was his face. His mother always said he had a face you could trust. And it was true; people were always anxious to tell him their deepest and darkest secrets. It was as if they could sense somehow that the information would be secure with James, that James, try as he might, could not tell untruths. Well, there was *something* in that. James did regularly confound his fellow bureaucrats with his honesty. It was a rare quality in Canberra and many people didn't know how to react. Either this James bloke was very, very intelligent or else hopelessly stupid. Generally it was much more convenient to believe the latter.

Their accommodation was modest: individual cinder block units, bunk beds, a lamp and some shelves—but it was functional and quite cool inside. James's biggest surprise was to walk outside and find a huge metal canister filled with water. He put his cup under the spigot and filled it, braving himself against the metallic flavour he expected. But the water was tremendous. He had never tasted better. Pumped up from some deep aquifer, purified by God knows what kind of filtering system—it might have been the best cup of water James had ever tasted. And out here, imagine—in the Red Centre!

Pam tapped James on the shoulder.

"Pam! Have you tasted the water? Here, try some!"

"Well actually, that's just what I was going to do. Did you know they have a swimming pool here?"

James sipped the water slowly. It deserved to be savoured, put on file with the most famous bins of the Hunter Valley. "A pool? Really?"

"Yeah," Pam pointed. "Over there. Thank God, eh? I don't know how I'd have got on in this heat otherwise." She was wearing a plain pink blouse, quite sheer. The heat had helped make it stick closely to her body and, in the day's late light, Pam's skin was radiant.

"I'd rather drink it than swim in it. Maybe later."

"All right," answered Pam, "suit yourself. I'll see *you*"—poking her finger in James's undefended chest—"*later*."

"Right."

Pam turned and walked away. She had a bounce to her step which suggested she was a dancer once, or an athlete—a firm, well-balanced body. James had to wipe off the water he had spilled on his chin.

CHAPTER THREE

T he rounded mountains which surrounded Canberra began to cast long shadows, spilling everywhere: into the streets and around tall buildings, creeping stealthily outwards, through the countryside, across the golden grain fields, through the acacias, around the trunks of eucalypts, flowing, inexorably with the certainty of an imam calling his people to prayer.

The evening sun hovered above the blue-green hills. Frank Peterson imagined the sound—the distant crackle, the sound of wood in a fireplace. The lowering sun became half a ball, now a crescent. Already there was a chill in the air as the last sliver of light disappeared. Night was upon them.

Frank drove his old red Torana up the winding road towards the Mt. Stromlo observatory. He was quite old for a graduate student which proved to be both an advantage and a liability. It made people question his intentions but, once they were satisfied in that regard, they accorded him a freedom and respect much harder won by his younger colleagues. After getting his MA in English literature, Frank had decided there was much more poetry in the stars than on the written page. The following term he had registered as a first year science student. That was six years ago. Frank would be thirty this winter.

It would be an hour yet before the sky would be dark enough for any serious work, so Frank didn't hurry. He sat down with the observatory's technician and leisurely discussed the evening's run. It was fairly straightforward stuff. Siding Springs tended to get all the really interesting work nowadays so proposals for Mt. Stromlo could afford to be a little more prosaic. Frank was doing what scores of colleagues had done before him. He was taking spectra of Eta Carinae to see if it had any more secrets to tell.

"So you're a grandfather now?" Frank asked.

"That's right. James Andrew's his name. Gets the Andrew from me." Andrew McMillan had been at Stromlo for as long as anyone could remember, had managed somehow to keep up with constant upgrades in equipment, moreover always knew where everything was and the shortest way to get anything done. This talent was not apparent from watching the man. He walked very deliberately and very slowly. Frank often wondered if it might be possible to upgrade *Andrew*, at least provide him with a new CPU, give him a few more megahertz to work with.

"Your first grandchild?"

"But not the last, I hope."

"And your daughter's in Perth, is it?"

"Perth, that's right."

"An awful long way to visit."

"Aye," answered Andrew staring gloomily into his cup. His tea was cold.

"Would you like me warm that up for you?" Frank asked.

"No, no, no." Andrew stretched and groaned simultaneously. "Well, let's get to work then, shall we? That's what they're paying us for."

Frank took both their cups to the sink and quickly washed them. Anxious as he was to get started, he lingered, straightening things, giving the counter a quick wipe. It was important to give Andrew all the time he needed.

"Eta Carinae, then, is it?" Andrew's voice echoed from across the room.

"Yes please."

The slit of the observatory dome opened as the large scope simultaneously moved through two axes. The sky showed a final splash of violet. Frank thought he caught a glimpse of Canopus as the dome turned.

From across the room, Andrew's voice called out, more quietly than usual, "Mr. Peterson."

"What is it, Andrew?"

"Come here, sir"

Frank had only just settled down at his computer and resented having to stop just as he had begun to type in instructions. "Is there some problem?"

"You tell me," Andrew pointed at the monitor.

"What am I looking at?"

" *That.*" Dozens of blobs of light filled the monitor and one of them should have been Eta Carinae. But something didn't look right. What was that *bright* object?

"You're sure you have the right field?" Andrew returned a stare of contempt. "No, sorry. Of course you're sure. Well, could it be a problem with the monitor?"

"Mr. Peterson," Andrew said, touching Frank's arm, "why don't we go out and have a look?"

As if in slow motion, Andrew rose from the chair and headed for the door, arriving there only after the passage of several geologic epochs. Yet Frank said nothing. Though his heart was pounding like a captured bird. Finally the door opened.

"There," said Andrew, stretching out a bony finger, "it looks like she's putting on a show for us."

"My God!" There it was, clearly visible. Eta Carinae, which should have been well below the threshold of visibility, gleamed before them as a more than respectable third magnitude object. It hadn't done something like this in—well, it must be a hundred and fifty years.

"Come on, Andrew, let's get that spectrum!"

Andrew turned slowly, in the middle of lighting a pipe. "Mr. Peterson ..." He puffed, enjoying the first moments of his little offering which rose to join the firmament. "We've waited all this time, we can wait a few minutes more."

CHAPTER FOUR

T he red earth gave way to the firmness of Uluru's back as, relentlessly, the Old Man, on hands and knees, led them higher.

"How much farther?" a young voice asked.

The Old Man put a finger to his lips.

The slope levelled out. Their pounding hearts beat like drums against the immensity of stars. There was sky on all sides: to the left, to the right, above, and even below—stars covering all the universe. They climbed and climbed until, over the last ridge, they met a ferocious, laughing wind. They walked on, buoyed by the wind, their necks craned up to view the great Milky Way. It was a giant serpent, one man whispered, a great river said another, a river, whispered a third, cloudy with flecks of gold.

James awoke suddenly, exhausted, having dreamt the whole night long. God, James, thought, must be something in the water. Quickly he slipped on some shorts—too quickly—almost tripping over himself when he couldn't find his left leg hole. Finally he made it outside. The day was brilliant, the sun already an hour into the sky, and Uluru, as always, stared back at him. It was a bizarre thought, but James could have sworn the monolith had somehow moved during the night.

Something was moving. In the distance. A dingo? It moved and then it stopped, then it moved again. The shadows were still long among the clumps of spinifex, so it was hard for James to tell what he was looking at. At times he thought he could hear a drone accompanying the movement, maybe even singing—but it couldn't—wait! Yes, they're people. They're aboriginals. What are they doing out there?

"Morning, James!"

"Cripes, Pam! You could tell someone you were coming!"

She was wearing a very long shirt of some kind—a nightgown James supposed. "Did I startle you?"

"I was just looking at something."

Pam put a hand to her forehead, shading her eyes from the sun.

"Out there. Do you see them?"

"Where?

"Over there." But they'd gone. "Well, they *were* there ... honestly ... some aboriginals. But I haven't the faintest idea what they were doing."

"Maybe you saw a dingo."

"No, no, there were at least a dozen of them. They seemed to be ... I don't know, hunting, stalking.... " A magpie landed on the corrugated roof of a neighbouring building. It looked at them and warbled, a call that made their hearts melt, leaving them momentarily speechless.

"You're here to see them aren't you?"

What the hell was she talking about?

Pam bent down to fasten the strap of her sandal. Her loose nightgown provided James an unencumbered view of her beautifully rounded breasts. Kata Djuta.

"I've been thinking about it," Pam continued. "The government must have sent you. You're here to negotiate with the aboriginals, right?"

The magpie too seemed to peer at Pamela's breasts. "Pam, I don't—"

"Well, come on then, time to get at it, isn't it?" Pam turned.

At it?

"There's one waiting for you right out front. Just let me change first. I'll only be a minute."

Pamela hurried back to her room. In her absence, the magpie flew down to the ground and occupied the spot she had vacated. It cocked its head and looked at James.

"Now I don't need any of that from you!" James had long had

the habit of talking to magpies. He'd tell his friends it was part of his aboriginal heritage but really it was more a personal quirk, something he'd always done since he was a little boy.

"All I did was *look*. A bloke's allowed to *look*."

The magpie turned away as if considering this proposition. In the end, it decided the only appropriate response was another one of its amazing warbles. It was so much a part of Australia—the song of the red rock, a sound which reminded James of a golden ball splashing at the bottom of some ancient well. It always quite undid him, evaporated from his mind all ordered thoughts, all words, sent him far back into time, into the dreaming …

The screen door of Pam's room slammed shut, but not before several bush flies rushed in. "Come on, James, this way!" How had she managed to change so fast? She had on a Dallas Cowboys singlet, some khaki shorts, and the same sandals. She also carried a large brimmed sun hat in her hand. "Come on, James!"

James. He liked the way she said his name: *Come on, James!* He was very good with voices and knew he had heard that exact intonation somewhere before, seen that exact body language … Yes, it was "Dr. No!" *Come on, James!* Who was that? Was it Ursula Andress? No, not her, someone else. Couldn't remember the name, but he could hear the voice, he could see the voluptuous figure—it was Pam…. *The name's Bond. James Bond.*

"Are you coming?" Pam had her hands on her hips.

"Yeah. I'll just get a shirt."

It was only a minute's walk to the hostel's lobby which was deserted except for the custodian. He was sweeping sand off the floor as if it were a job assigned to him for eternity. "G'day" James said as they rushed by. "G'day," the custodian answered back, the venom only a short distance from his lips. He threw his finished cigarette butt onto the floor and crushed it out of existence.

"Well, here we are then." Pam waved to a tall black elder who stood just outside the lobby, beneath a neighbouring desert oak. It was difficult to guess his age. He had lost some hair from the top of his head and his beard was grey. Yet he had a strong and lean torso. There was no hint of softness, no wasted tissue. He was as strong as it made sense for him to be. Adorned only by a loin cloth and a string of stones which hung around his neck, he presented an image of considerable power. His eyes seemed far too bright for his dark body. James thought he had never seen anyone stand so erect.

Two naked children ran in circles around the tree, laughing. Hidden deeper in the shade was a woman, breast-feeding an infant.

"G'day," James said to the man.

"This is Billy, Pam explained, "well, that's not his real name, but he says you can call him that because you wouldn't be able to pronounce his aboriginal name."

"What are you talking about, Pam?" James snickered, unable to stop himself. "Do you know this man? Have you met him before?"

"Well, not before this morning. But I think I know his cousin."

Again James snickered, kicking himself immediately after. Why did he ask so many stupid questions "What's this all about, Pam?"

Billy then spoke in his native tongue, an odd language to English ears, liberally sprinkled with clicks, musical in a very non-Western way. It was a combination of sounds which James had only ever heard in TV documentaries.

"Billy says he's been waiting for you—he's glad you've come."

"You *understand* him?"

"Sure."

"I thought you were a journalist?"

Pam smiled. "I thought you thought that."

"Well how is it you—I mean you're—"

"You mean how is it a white girl can speak Pitjantajara?"

"Yeah."

"I'm an anthropologist, James. Well, at least I hope to be. Pitjantajara is my speciality. I doing my thesis on it."

"Geez, Pam, you really had me going!"

Pam winked at him, then Billy spoke again.

"He wants you to go walkabout with him."

"Me?"

"He says there's some important things you have to see."

James felt he was losing his balance, looked around for a place he might lean against. "Well, tell him—tell him, I'm honoured. I would love to go on a walkabout with him, but tell him first we have some pressing business to discuss. Tell him I represent the government in Canberra."

"Billy knows that."

"He knows that?"

Pam shrugged. "He says he dreamed about you."

"What?" James tried to shoo away the flies which were circling his head. "Bloody flies!"

Billy rose to his feet. His family joined him.

"Well," said Pam, again with hands on her hips, "are you coming?"

"Coming?" Totally flummoxed, James laughed. "Where?"

"Geez you can be a little dense, James. Canberra-disease, I reckon?"

Billy raised his walking stick and pointed off in the distance toward Kata Djuta. Despite what James had said earlier, it had to be *twenty-five* kilometres, not fifteen. Maybe thirty. "I suppose we're going to walk?"

Pam smiled. "You going to put on a hat?"

CHAPTER FIVE

Patrick Mahoney sipped a daiquiri from poolside. Global warming be damned, it was only now that it had finally warmed up to a respectable Queensland temperature and appropriately now there were three topless women on lounges opposite him. The Minister watched with satisfaction: any longer on their stomachs and their backs would turn to a crisp—couldn't have that now, could we?

Ah, it was a wonderful, wonderful day—a great day to be in the Whitsundays—that is until a lorikeet shat on the Minister, and almost simultaneously his cell phone rang, suggesting a very odd cause-and-effect relationship.

"Shit! What is this stuff?"

Six breasts turned simultaneously.

"Shit!" The phone rang insistently, six or seven times, 'til finally the Minister, having had barely time to wipe himself, answered his call. "Now what is it?"

It did not matter that the voice on the other end of the line spoke as if tip-toeing through a minefield—no caller, this day, would be spared the Minister's wrath.

"Well that's fine, Jimmy boy, I'm glad you're getting on with your relatives, but what about the BLOODY BLOCKADE?" The young women opposite listened with a newborn interest. It hadn't occurred to them that this curious little man might be someone important.

"Did I miss something, Jimmy? You're going on walkabout *because* ...?"

One of the young women got up and stretched—slowly, languorously—heading for the deep end of the pool.

"And what the hell has a bloody star got to do with it?"

The young woman bent over to feel the temperature of the water.

"Yeah, yeah, I have a biro—okay, tell me again. Eta?"

She slipped her legs into the water, a little spasm running up the length of her body. She had developed a nice tan over the last week and her reflection in the water was quite fetching.

"Eta what? Carina? Carin-*eye*. Whatever ... All right, but I have to tell *you*, Jimmy boy, this had *better* be important."

A voice called out from one of the lounge chairs, "How's the water, Crystal?" The Minister glanced over. Imagine parents naming their kids after some soap opera star— bloody outrageous —why don't you just get in the water, Crystal! Am I the only around here who has any sense of *time management*?

"Look, Jimmy, just in case someone asks, the bloke's name is what again? Billy?" A pause. Would the Minister explode? No one could tell. "That's it?"

James offered to find out his Pitjantajara name.

"No, no, don't bother, mate." Shaking his head, the Minister glanced towards the pool. By now, Crystal was halfway in. The Minister took note, and Crystal noticed him noticing.

"Look, I don't know how long you plan to spend down there, but I'm expecting some news ASAP. So find out from that Billy person what they want, and let's get that place re-opened."

With a final shiver, Crystal fully immersed herself in the pool. With strong, luxurious strokes she made her away across its length and then returned doing the backstroke. It was, the Minister instantly decided, his favourite stroke.

"Look, I have to go, mate. Call me again when you have something to report, something important. What? No, I won't forget about bloody Eta Carina!"

Putting down his phone, the Minister slowly rose from his lounge chair. "Geez," he said, slapping his hands on his ample hips, "it's getting like a furnace out here."

CHAPTER SIX

They had walked for two hours, and Kata Djuta did not seem appreciably closer. Nor had the blood-redness of the land paled in the least. Come to me, it seemed to call. Make your blood and mine co-mingle....

"I have to tell you, Pam, the Minister didn't sound too happy."

Pam smiled. "From what I've seen of him on the telly, he's never too happy, is he?"

"Sad, but true." James could hear his boots crunch in the sand. Is this what it sounds like walking in snow?

"All the same, Pam, it's hardly my role, is it? Telling the Minister to point a telescope towards some star neither of us has even heard of."

"You told him it was important?"

"Pam, it's not like he holds my word in high regard or anything. Anyway, how do I know it's important? How do I know it just isn't some aboriginal ... mumbo-jumbo? I've only got Billy's word for it."

Pam stopped, stared.

"What?"

"Don't move."

Oh God, I hope she's not asking herself how one aboriginal could be distrustful of another?

Suddenly Pam's hand shot out and knocked something off James's shoulder.

"It was just a *huntsman*. Could give you a nasty bite, but it wouldn't kill you, not like a *funnel-web*. You'll be right."

James saw only half a second of the spider before it darted behind a rock. It was as big as his fist. Catching his breath, checking to see if he had spit left to swallow, James managed,

"Thanks, Pam," all the while marvelling that somehow his knees were not visibly shaking.

"I used to collect spiders when I was a girl."

No surprise there.

"My favourites were the trap-door spiders."

Soon they stopped under a ghost gum to rest. James had never been anywhere so quiet. Apart from bush flies, which continued to circle his head like little Spitfires, it was silent. Once he thought he heard a breeze, but when he looked up, the leaves were still. They had wandered far from the road—there was no evidence that this landscape had ever seen vehicles, or any other accoutrements of civilization. Only the vapour trail of a jet heading towards Perth marred the perfect blueness of the sky.

Billy walked over to a nearby bush and brushed his fingers along a flower stem. A thick translucent liquid oozed onto his fingers.

"You ever try it?" Pam asked. "Honey Grevillea. Here—like this. Just run your thumb and forefinger along the flower stock and gather up the nectar." Pam demonstrated and held her fingers out towards James.

Did she expect him to lick them?

Finally Pam took James's hand for him and ran his startled fingers along the stock. At Pam's signal, they both put their fingers in their mouths.

"Good, eh?"

"Wonderful!"

They returned for more, laughed as they fell into a synchronous rhythm, both bringing fingers to their mouths at the same time.

"What did you call this stuff?"

Honey Grevillea

Billy was now resting his head against the bark of the gum tree, apparently asleep.

The nectar was incredible. James had never felt so refreshed. He felt like he should leap skyward or, at the very least, do some one-handed push-ups à la Jack Palance. "So, Pam, what do we do now?"

"Rest." Pam immediately stretched out and put the sun hat over her face. James watched her chest rise up and down.

"But I'm not tired."

"Well, no one's going anywhere in this heat. You might as well rest while you can."

"I can't. Seems all I've been doing lately is resting, dreaming. I guess I'll just sit up and look around for a bit."

"Suit yourself."

With exquisite rhythm, as if marking the pulse of all the universe, Pam's chest rose, remained suspended, then fell gently down. And so it had always done, since the very beginning, since the dreamtime when Pun d-jel *the Creator formed a man and woman out of the desert clay. Then, holding them by the shoulders,*

Pun d-jel blew breath into their mouths, then into their noses and finally into their navels. Then the Creator rose up and began to dance, and in his dancing he brought his new creations to life. The man and women then stood up, wiped themselves off and, after looking around for a few minutes, they moved their lips and spoke.

Pam momentarily interrupted the rhythm of the galaxy and lifted the hat from her eyes. "See if you can catch us a goanna for dinner, okay James?"

"What?"

"Gotcha."

Pam laughed. At the same moment a breeze moved through the foliage. James suddenly knew that there was no combination of sounds in all the world more pleasant than this.

CHAPTER SEVEN

Frank and Andrew had worked all through the night; they took spectra, they sent e-mail, they made telephone calls; their routine had grown to a frenzy that might never be topped in their careers. Even after Eta Carinae had finally set below the horizon, Andrew could not be persuaded to go home. Only reluctantly had he agreed to catch an hour's nap on the sofa in the office. Frank tried to sleep also, but had no better luck. He was waiting to hear back from a colleague in South Africa. In his head, he kept replaying their initial telephone conversation. Despite Telecom's advertising, the line had been poor.

"Yes, yes, it shows all the classic signs of being a Type I supernova! Yes, I'm sure. Well, you'll have to look for yourself, but it's not like you can miss it."

Frank always had trouble with the Afrikaner accent. He only understood half of what his colleague said in reply.

"You'll phone us back then? E-mail? Yes e-mail is fine. You have our address? Good, good. And how many hours there before Carina is up? Yes, yes, well, we'll just have to wait, then. Thank you so much. What? What? Oh, just blind good luck, I guess. But thanks! Well, I await your call then. G'day."

Almost everything in the observatory was digital, yet an old-fashioned analogue clock still hung in the office. Frank could hear it ticking. He went over to investigate and was surprised to see that he could actually see the minute hand moving. He hadn't thought that possible. It wasn't just that he saw it move in small discrete jerks. He could see it move smoothly and continuously between each of the minute marks. He watched the hand move closer and closer to the top of the clock, in his mind, counting down, as if in preparation for a space launch. Ten, nine, eight, seven—in five seconds it will be precisely six o'clock. But then, much to Frank's surprise, the clock made one hell of an unusual sound.

It was the phone!

Kata Djuta

CHAPTER EIGHT

It was late afternoon, and Kata Djuta loomed on the horizon like bloody knuckles which had punched through the sand. Its walls formed grand and complex cathedrals, a maze of red and brown conglomerate, from this distance smooth, rounded and polished by the wind.

"How much longer?"

"Billy thinks maybe an hour, probably two hours for you."

"Thanks for the vote of confidence." James wiped the perspiration off his forehead. Why wasn't anyone else sweating? "Have you any idea what we're going to see?"

"No."

No? That's it? You wouldn't care to elaborate? Surely Pam must have more to say on the subject than *that*....

Quiet was an unusual quality in white girl although common among James's relatives. When James's cousins were over for visits, they might spend an hour together and not say a word. It was a habit James had gradually lost—wasn't of much use in Canberra where you were expected to talk all the time even if you had nothing to say.

James's mother would have liked Pam.

> *"So you've got yourself a white girl, James?"*
>
> *"She's really nice, mom. She even speaks Pitjantajara, can you imagine?"*
>
> *"Does she? She's very talented then?"*
>
> *"Yes, mom. She seems to be. She's an anthropologist."*
>
> *"Oh, one of those ... and I suppose she'd bear you lots of blue-eyed children, would she?"*

"We've only just met, mom."

A large goanna scurried out from a clump of spinifex, in pursuit of a kangaroo rat. James's mouth was too dry to make more than a feeble cry. The goanna was even bigger than the one he'd seen from the bus. "God!" he yelled weakly, then recovering himself, "there goes dinner!"

Billy opened his eyes and on all fours crawled over to examine the tracks left by the goanna. He sat very still. Finally he spoke to Pam.

"What did he say?"

"The goanna is Billy's mood-jin-garl, his totem."

"And seeing him is *good*, right?"

"It depends. The goanna is Billy's protector, and often appears when there's danger."

"Then it's *not* good."

"It's not that exactly; sometimes the goanna appears as a sign of affirmation too. That's what he's done this time. That's what Billy thinks."

"And what exactly does Billy think is being affirmed?"

"You, of course."

"Pardon?"

"It means that's it's okay for you to continue the walkabout."

James looked back at the distance he had travelled. Uluru was now a small bump on the horizon. "You mean there was some doubt?"

James's heart melted as Pam laughed in reply.

Mr. Stromlo Observatory

CHAPTER NINE

Everyone in the Department of Astronomy was at the Mt. Stromlo Observatory. In fact, there were many present who, strictly speaking, were not in the Department at all. The allure of a celestial cataclysm was just too great. In a strange twist of fate, a small system of bad weather hovered over Siding Springs, so there was even a contingent of astronomers who had flown in from there. They seemed just a bit perturbed not to be the centre of attention, but they too were quickly caught up in the excitement.

"Gentlemen! Gentlemen!" Gradually the hubbub began to subside. Greg waited for just the right moment. "I beg your pardon —*ladies* and gentlemen—if I may have your attention ..."

"That's right, Greg, there are such things as female astronomers!" There was laughter from the crowd, just a sprinkling of it feminine.

"Of course! Some of the finest in our field are drawn from the fairer sex and who would deny that we are the better for it?"

"Just get on with it, for God's sake," an anonymous voice uttered, but the comment was largely swallowed up by the crowd.

"This afternoon we are here to commemorate the beginning of a great event."

Plenty of *hear, hears* from the crowd.

Greg Follows was the Head of Astronomy and this was a moment he had dreamed of all his life. At sixty, he still had a full head of hair which, though snow white, spoke of a virility and energy which was more than superficial. Greg surfed in the summer, skied in the winter. He was strong, intelligent, and absolutely ruthless.

"We have waited a long time for this, my friends—not since the 17th century have we had a supernova in our backyard—with apologies to SN1987, of course...."

Guffaws from the crowd—the 1987 supernova had been 160 thousand light years away! Studying it was like kissing your sister.

"But now," Greg continued, "the moment has finally come, and how fitting that it should first be discovered in Australia and by one of own colleagues. I'm sure you would all like to join me congratulating Jim—no, *Frank! Frank* Peterson for his brilliant work!"

Frank raised a meek hand and waved at the crowd. "Don't forget Andrew!"

Andrew was nowhere to be seen. He didn't want strangers anywhere near his equipment and refused to budge from his office. Moreover, he said, he was thinking of going to Perth for a holiday. ASAP.

Greg asked, "What's the magnitude now, Frank?"

"Three hours ago, South Africa reported second magnitude, well on its way to one. At this rate it'll be as bright as Venus by week's end."

As bright as Venus! The excitement rippled through the crowd. Greg realized it would be futile to try to speak over the resurgent noise so instead he went over to visit Margaret.

"Maggie! So glad you could make it!"

"Just try to keep me away." Maggie's face hurt from all the smiling she had already done and was yet expected to do.

Greg leaned closer, eyebrows narrowed, his face concerned and rather too sympathetic. "Hell of thing, Maggie, the way the weather turned on you...."

"Oh come on, Greg, the fact that Siding Springs is socked in is the best thing that could have happened, isn't it?"

"Maggie, you do me wrong ..."

Margaret almost choked on her drink.

"To cast me off discourteously...."

"Oh don't sing, For God's sake, Greg! Show *some* mercy!"

"As madam wishes." The Head of Astronomy smiled. He

preferred to keep his supply of *bon mots* for more fertile ground. He jiggled his drink. He began to look around for an excuse to leave, but Margaret had no intention of making it *that* easy.

"Well, I *am* impressed, Greg. You have this reception beautifully organized, as always."

"It was nothing."

"How you managed to arrange all this on such short notice, I can't imagine. It's almost as if you knew all along this was going to happen."

Greg sipped on his drink. "You know, I did receive this unusual telephone call around eleven o'clock this morning." By force of habit, Greg looked around him, making sure no one would overhear his remarks, or perhaps making sure that just the right person would. "From the Minister for Parks and Aboriginal Affairs —you know, what's his name?"

"Mahoney?"

"Thank you. Well anyway, he tells me someone instructed him to tell us to turn our telescopes towards Eta Carinae—he butchered the pronunciation, of course—sort of an anonymous tip."

"You're joking?"

"Some aboriginal person—some elder—told him to take a good look at Eta Carinae."

"And you got this message this morning?"

"Yes, late this morning. Mind you, Frank had detected the object twelve hours before, so there's no doubt about who has the prior claim for discovery."

The ice cubes in Greg's drink clinked together with unusual loudness.

"What do you make of it, Greg?"

"A hoax I suppose—not too malicious as hoaxes go, thankfully."

"But how would an aboriginal elder have any idea?"

"Search me." Greg's eyes again began to wander around the room. He hadn't really meant to tell this story to Margaret.

"Margaret! Margaret! Over here!" Blessed relief. The call came from the opposite corner where Frank and a colleague, named

Felix, stood waving.

Just as Margaret stood out for being only one of two women in the crowd, Felix stood out as the observatory's lone East Indian. He was often mistaken for an aboriginal. When this happened, Felix laughed hysterically.

"Margaret, isn't it wonderful!" Felix was never anything but enthusiastic. He left no margin for raising his elation to higher levels for events like this. "Just think, in our own lifetimes—that it should be *us* to witness the cataclysm. How incredibly fortunate for us!"

"I remember in school," Frank said, "we had this teacher who was crazy about the stars—he's the one who really got me interested, I reckon—anyway he kept telling us that one day Betelgeuse was going to explode and that if we were very lucky we might see it happen."

"It might yet, Frank!" It seemed like Felix would float to the ceiling if he were not held down. "Wouldn't that be something? Two supernovas in one lifetime!"

Margaret liked Felix. His enthusiasm and general optimism about things was very appealing. And if his colour and accent weren't enough to set him apart, he was a professed Christian, who believed quite literally that the Creator played an active and compassionate role in the drama of the universe. He believed the universe had a *purpose*. Margaret sometimes wished *she* could believe in such a fairy tale. "It's not unheard of, Felix. Kepler saw two supernovas, or was it three?"

"It was two," Frank answered—hesitantly—after all he was only a grad-student, "just two."

"Two!" Felix exclaimed. "Can you imagine that? And I'm this excited over just one! You'll excuse me, Frank, Margaret, but I just love those little sausage things. I must get some before they're all gone. Shall I get some for you?"

"No, no thanks."

"Margaret?"

"They give me gas, Felix."

"Oh my, well, we mustn't do that! I won't be a moment!" Felix dove bravely into the crowd, speaking to colleagues continuously as he dodged in and out.

"So Frank, I guess they've shoved you out, have they?"

"Actually, Maggie, they've been pretty decent about it. They've called in Hollis, of course, and Cooper, but they've invited me to work with them. Greg said it would be good PR for me to continue on the project."

Margaret could no longer spot Greg in the crowd. "That old bastard—in spite of himself, he ends up doing the right thing once in a while. Well that's great, Frank, I'm really happy for you. You should have one hell of a thesis when this is all over."

"Thanks," said Frank. "I mean, I hope so." Frank paused, checked the polish on his shoes, then took the plunge. "Look, Margaret, this is probably a stupid question, but has any one ever done any work on the possible effects of a supernova exploding this close to us?"

"What do you mean?"

"It's just that when those heavy particles start arriving in a few weeks time—well, they might not be all that wonderful for our atmosphere. I don't know—I'm just speculating."

Margaret put down her empty glass. "The atmosphere did just fine when Kepler was around...."

"That's true, but those stars were further away, at least twice as far—there might be a critical threshold. I know it's a stupid thought, but I just wondered...."

Margaret looked into her purse for a calculator. Too many compartments. "No, no, it's not stupid at all. Actually, this is right up Felix's line. Has he got his sausages yet? Felix! Felix! Over here!"

Felix saw them. He waved his full hands and began gingerly navigating his way through the crowd. "I brought some extras, just in case you changed your mind!"

"Felix, look at these figures and tell me what you think."

Felix put down the sausages and gazed deeply into the nebula of numbers. "Holy Mother of God," he said, whistling lowly, "what have we here?"

Soon it was as if Felix had forever lived in a universe quite devoid of tasty appetizers.

Kata Djuta

CHAPTER TEN

ow that they were close, James could see how
geologically complex Kata Djuta was. It was far from
being a uniform colour. It displayed many hues of red
and brown, and white and black mineral stains showed where
transient waterfalls had once flowed. Many of the rock walls
were peppered with fist-sized conglomerates. In other places it
was smooth, the bedding largely horizontal, unlike Uluru. Most
fascinating of all was the lush vegetation which grew in protected
valleys between the cliffs—micro-worlds, harbouring who knows
what strange and ancient creatures.

The sun now hovered low in the west, making all the land
(almost unbelievably) redder. Like a broken egg-yolk, the solar
disk spilled the last of its colour over the great outback and the
ground soaked it up in grateful silence.

"Just a little further," Pam explained. She removed her sun hat
and shook loose her long head of hair. "We're going to make camp
over by that creek."

James could hear the delicate sound of water wrapping its
fingers around the sandstone pebbles, the mini-waterfalls, the
leaves which floated on its surface—even the tread of water
beetles—it all seemed tangible, irresistible. The gentlest of winds
shook the leaves of the nearby gums.

"Billy wants us to gather some kindling. Come on."

All day long, James had been hot, unbearably so. It didn't seem
possible there could be a time in this same twenty-four period
when he would be cold, but even now, he began to shiver. The
western sky was golden, melting quickly into hues of green,
indigo and violet, and with the colour change all the heat of the

day rushed skyward, back to the place from which it came.

"Don't we need a permit or something to burn fires here?"

"Don't be an idiot, James."

"I do work for the Parks Department, Pam. I'm sure I remember issuing permits for this sort of thing."

"So *you're* the bloke always giving us a hard time!"

"Well, it isn't me *personally.* I countersign the paper sometimes, but it's actually somebody else who—"

Pam walked right up to James, nose to nose, her arms already filled with wood.

"James? Did anybody ever tell you, you have a tendency to go on and on about things?"

That's it? That's the extent of her criticism? "Well, yes, Pam, people have noted it from time to time, now that you mention—"

James was stopped by a kiss on the mouth.

"Come on, James, let's get this fire going before it gets dark."

CHAPTER ELEVEN

The fire hissed and crackled. A small blue flame licked the surface of the wood and the surrounding cliffs stood over them like giant ancestors, making sure no observance should be missed. To James the bogey man had never seemed so palpable.

Once again he could see himself in the back of his Uncle's wagon, the moon as big as a cartwheel, bobbing up and down along the creaking hill. His mother held him in her arms to keep away the chill and, in hushed tones, they dared to speak of Najara.

> *"How does Najara find the little boys, mom?"*
> *"He is very clever, Najara is. He knows the ways of little boys. He hides in the tall grass or behind a dune of sand and he whistles."*
> *"He whistles?"*
> *"That's right." His mother nodded. "Like this." Then she whistled a few haunting phrases till her son's eyes were like two rising moons.*
> *"A boy becomes mesmerized when he hears this tune, and walks into the desert to look for it."*
> *HE would never do such a thing, James promised himself.*
> *"And when the boy comes close enough, Najara grabs him and runs off with him and keeps him forever. Such boys forget their language and tribe and are never heard from again."*
> *The air was windless and James could hear the cicadas and every creak of the cartwheels.*

"James?"
"What?!"

Pam laughed. "I didn't mean to startle you!" Her voice was like the sound of the creek running. "Geez, you're easily spooked aren't you?"

"I was daydreaming, or ... something." The front of James was warm by the fire, but his back was freezing.

"Billy thinks you're ready now."

"Ready?"

Pam rolled her eyes. "For the lesson."

"Is he going to teach me about witchity grubs or something?" It was stupid thing to say. He wondered if Pam could see his sheepish smile in the firelight.

"All right," James said. "I guess I'm as ready as I'll ever be."

Billy moved over to sit beside James. James was amazed to discover that Billy smelled—well, how else could he describe it except *good*? No one who had walked all day in the desert and not bathed, so far as he could tell, could possibly smell so *good.* It was a mystery that needed further consideration. Pam moved close to him on the other side. She too smelled good.

Billy spoke and pointed at the sky. Pam translated.

"There were seven sisters of the Bunjalung tribe. They were beautiful and clever and their digging sticks were very powerful. At their ends were special charms which could perform heaps of magic." Billy paused and gazed longingly up at the cluster of stars Westerners call the Pleiades.

"One day, one of the sisters was attracted by a goanna and strayed from the rest of the group. Karambal had been watching her and decided he would take her for his wife. Yet this was not allowed for she was of the wrong kin for him to marry. Nevertheless he captured her."

James had heard a story vaguely like this once before, but he didn't remember how it ended.

Pam had inched even closer to James and James could feel her shoulder brush against his as Billy resumed talking.

"The other sisters found out what happened and thought of ways to free their sister. Finally they decided to travel to the west and bring back Winter. 'We will unleash Winter,' they said. 'That will make Karambal free our sister.' The sister was safe from the effects of the cold by her special magic, but Karambal almost froze to death, he and all his tribe. It did not take long before Karambal complied and let the sister go."

Billy paused. But his eyes never left the sky. It was as if he were examining each tiny star and unravelling from it more and more details of the story.

"When their sister returned, the women of Bunjalung journeyed east to bring back Summer. While they were there, they thought they would make springs at the heads of all the mountain rivers. And that is what they did. And they brought back Summer. Then they went to live in the stars."

Billy stopped. He wrapped his hands behind his neck and breathed deeply.

What now, James wondered, looking over to Pam whose expression offered no help whatsoever. What *was* the protocol after such a thing? Finally James said, "That's a lovely story." He had to say *something*. "So when we see those stars, what do we call them?"

"Monkira," Pam replied, "the Pleiades."

"So when we see the Pleiades, that means summer is returning, right? I think my Uncle told me that."

Pam smiled. The shadows were deep in her face, and all the landscape around them. The mystery deepened when, seemingly out of nowhere, a can of hot water appeared. They would soon have tea. Desert magic.

"And when the Seven Sisters disappear in the West," Pam continued, "that means winter is near—to remind us not marry into the wrong clan."

"So the whole story's about marriage taboos, then?"

"Hardly!" Pam laughed. "Ready for tea?"

"Am I! Please."

For the next half hour they mostly sat in silence. With the tea and fire, they were warmed right to tips of their toes and comforted by the cry of distant dingoes, first violins in the desert orchestra, who seemed to sing out in salute to the everlasting stars.

"You know, James, there's more to that story."

"Why am I not surprised?"

"That Karambal was a bit of a scoundrel, it seems."

"Don't tell me he—"

"Well, he had enough sense to leave the *sisters* alone, but for his next conquest he chose a woman who was already married."

"Bloody hell."

"Well, it was, rather. The husband chased him day and night and finally found him hiding atop a tall gum tree. So he set fire to the tree."

"So that, I reckon, was the end of Karambal?"

"Not quite. The gods placed him in the sky, right beside Monkira —the Seven Sisters." Pam pointed. "You see? There he is, that orange coloured star. I think it's called Aldebaran."

"So, that's Karambal. Poor bugger...." James sipped on his tea. It's true what his mother always said, everything tastes better in the bush. "He's left hanging up there, always in sight of the sisters but never within reach. Frustrated for eternity."

"That's a pretty chauvinistic interpretation!" Pam kicked some sand at him.

"Hey! You've got sand in my tea!"

"Careful you, or we might just find a place for you up there with Karambal!" James pulled Pam to the ground, knocking over their tea in the process. They laughed and feigned outrage and each delighted in the other's texture. Had they not been otherwise occupied, James and Pam would have noticed a splendid meteor streaking through the constellation Eridanus.

The Keyhole Nebula in the constellation Carina

CHAPTER TWELVE

With an organizational flair typical of him, Greg had arranged for three large monitors to be hooked up to the observatory's computers. One showed a live visual image of the new supernova; a second, the projected brightness graph; and a third, the latest spectra from Eta Carinae. Only the news reporters paid attention to the visual image. Most of the astronomers stayed close to the spectra, oohing and ahhing when they recognized the signature of their favourite element.

Felix, Margaret, and Frank had retreated to the kitchen area and leaned their heads close together over the table.

"So what are you saying?" Margaret asked. "Are you saying the heavy particles are going to strip away the insulating molecules in our atmosphere?"

It was a struggle for Frank to get the words out—the last thing he wanted was to come off as some kind of *galah*. "What I'm saying is that's it's *possible*. Maybe worth looking into."

"Oh, I'd say it's a little more than possible, my friend." Felix patted Frank on the back. It struck Frank as a strange gesture —a little like shaking the hand of a man who just invented the guillotine. "If all these projections prove true, I'm afraid our atmosphere is in for some serious frying." Felix wrote figures as he spoke. He was one of those rare men who truly could do two or three things at once.

"Well, how close is it?" Margaret asked.

"Estimates keep changing, but my best guess puts the supernova at about 6300 light years. That's the figure we're working with."

"That's close."

"It's almost three times closer than Tycho's star."

"Well," said Margaret, "the question is how close is *too* close."

"Yes," said Felix, smiling, "that *is* the sixty-four thousand dollar question." Felix paused in his work for the first time in hours. "Is it possible for a bloke to find some tea in this place?"

"Sure," Frank answered.

"Don't move, Mr. Peterson, I'll get it."

"Andrew, you don't have to—"

"No, no, no. Can't bloody well do much with all these interlopers here, but I *can* make tea."

"Please, Andrew—"

"No, no, I don't mind." It was too late; Andrew had already begun his trek.

Frank felt bad; he had forgotten all about his elderly colleague who, until now, had been sitting in the corner arranging a photo album.

Frank turned to the others, sighing. It wasn't the most politic thing to do, but he had to tell someone. "You know, there's some evidence for global impact in the past."

Felix's eyes opened wide.

"Well, I know global climate is incredibly complex, and its a little naive to point to one factor but …"

"But what?" asked Margaret, finishing the last of the sausage hors d'oeuvres that Felix had brought back with him. "Go on, Frank. You've stuck your neck out this far."

Damn right. "You've heard of the *Little Ice Age,* Margaret?"

"Sure."

"The thing is, there's a pretty well-documented period of global cooling which started around 1560 and lasted to 1700 and—"

Margaret completed the thought for him. "And those dates correspond closely with the explosion of Kepler's two supernova…. Hmph."

As was the case for almost everyone, Frank didn't know how to read Margaret's expression. Oh God, he thought.

"You're right of course," Margaret said finally, "triggers for climate change are almost impossible to pin down."

Already Frank was sorry he had brought it up.

"All the same…" Margaret smiled. "You're not trying to write *two* theses, are you? Frank, you really must leave *something* for those other post-grads to do."

"It's just a thought, I—"

Margaret stepped closer to him, almost nose to nose. Frank was surprised to notice Margaret was wearing perfume. "What I'd like to know," Margaret asked, "is how you came up with this idea."

"What do you mean?"

"Well, I mean for the rest of them in there, it's simply a carnival, isn't it? It's like they're standing around watching a house on fire and wondering when the roof will collapse. Or, like Greg, they're wondering how this event can advance their careers. The best you can say about most of them is they're wondering how Eta Carinae is going to effect their work—but *their* work, only. It doesn't seem like anybody else is taking a global view of this thing."

"Well thanks, but I'm not quite so noble as you make me out to be."

"No?"

"I read it in a book. *Inferno*—years ago. You know, by Fred Hoyle —it was about this very thing: what might happen if a supernova exploded close to us. Well, actually, it was a quasar in Hoyle's case. At least, we're not dealing with a quasar, we can be thankful for that."

"Ah … " Felix said, knowingly, "Fred Hoyle."

"I know he's regarded as bit of a flake—that's why I was reluctant—"

"Fred Hoyle is no flake—or what is it you Australians say? No galah! On the contrary. My father met Mr. Hoyle once … a fine man, sort of the James Dean of Astronomy!"

"Then you don't think the whole idea is ridiculous?"

"Goodness no! I don't know that there's much we can *do* about it, mind you, but the science is fascinating, Frank. Positively fascinating! Do you think we can set up a simulation on the CRAY in Canberra?"

"Might be tricky. I'll have to check with Cooper. "

There was a change in the background noise, not so much the volume as the rhythm and pitch; people were making their good-byes. "Look," said Margaret, "I better check again to see what the weather's like at Siding Springs." Margaret took out her cell phone.

No one had noticed Andrew who, for the last minute, had been slowly approaching them. "Ladies and gentlemen," he said, "tea is served."

CHAPTER THIRTEEN

For hours, Billy told stories. All the constellations had them, even the great swath of the Milky Way, which in its patches of dark and light held ancient tales, the wisdom of a race, perhaps of a species. James listened to all Billy had to say, transfixed, eventually resting his head on the ground next to Pam. He gazed upward, not sure if he was awake or dreaming.

"It is the smoke from Nagacork's campfire," Billy explained via Pam. "There he lies with his beautiful lubra, his arm behind her head, gazing at the faraway light of other campfires in other lands. Maybe tonight he sees our campfire too." Pam smiled as she finished the translation. James could hear the smile.

He had put his arm in the same position as Nagacork. It was growing numb from lack of circulation, but damned if he was going to move it. Pam turned and nibbled on his ear.

"Oh!" James yelled, sitting up.

"What?"

He had to think quickly. "It's my arm. It's gone asleep." James shook his arm, hoping to make it appear rubbery.

"Let me rub it for you."

"No, Pam, you don't have to—"

"No, no, come on ..." Pam began to massage James's arm and kissed his ear while she was about it.

"Pam," James said, "I still don't know what this is all about. I mean, it's been great—to come out here, to learn all the stories, and best of all to be with you, but, I still don't see the point. I mean, I have this job to do—I can't get out of it. Do you think now that Billy's finished with the lesson, we can start negotiating?"

Pam paused a long time before she spoke. She was downright

aboriginal in this habit and it made James want to scream. "You like your job, do you, James?"

"Well ... yes, Pam. I reckon I do. But I'm not too likely to keep it if I don't do what I'm told. I need to ask Billy some questions."

Pam let go of James's arm and kissed him on the cheek. "All right, Mr. Canberra, let's ask him."

James noticed that the Southern Cross was well up and beside it he could see a dark patch, relatively devoid of stars. What did they call that? And then over to the left was a magnificent conglomeration of stars, whole knots of them, clusters, swarms. There must be a name for them. James broke a stick and threw it into the fire.

"Billy said you may ask him questions."

"Well, finally—good." Pam sat down beside him, held her knees up to her chest and wrapped her arms tightly around them.

"Billy, first I want to thank you for this magnificent walkabout. It has been a privilege and honour to accompany you. I have learned many things."

As usual, Pam translated.

"So?" James asked, "did you tell him all that?"

"Yes."

"And?"

"And what?"

"Doesn't he have anything to say in reply—you know, any ..."

"You expect him to say *you're welcome?*"

"Well, no, not if he doesn't want to—ah, forget it."

James shook his head, cleared his throat. Anything he had ever learned about protocol was worthless out here.

"All right then, here's the first question. Ask Billy, if you would, why his people have closed the park."

Flames stood between Billy and James, periodically obscuring their faces, but James was sure he could see the old man smiling.

"Billy says the park is not closed. He wonders how anyone can close a park?"

"Well, you know what I mean. Then ask him why the airport is closed, what plans do his people have for Uluru?"

It took Billy a long time to answer. More than once, Pam asked him follow-up questions to clarify the response. At last Pam turned again to James.

"This will be difficult to explain.... Billy says in normal times the white man is invited to Uluru as his guest. He is treated with respect and honour though these things are not always given back in return. He says the Pitjantajara always hope that one day the white man will learn that he belongs to the world, not the other way around. And so the Pitjantajara have waited patiently. But all things come to an end."

James could vividly see the Minister yelling at him.

"Billy says these are not normal times, and the guests must go to their own home and prepare as they think best."

"Prepare for what?"

Pam asked another question of Billy. He answered with words and a gesture.

"He calls it the Great Change." Billy interrupted her—"No, more like the Great Cooling or the Great Heating—the words are ambiguous."

"What? You mean like global warming?"

"No. Much bigger than that."

"Well, what then?"

Pam shrugged her shoulders. Billy elaborated.

"Billy says that this is his home. And now they must have privacy in their home, so they may prepare for the ... the Great ... Change. They must ... clean themselves ... and they must pray. There must be no distractions."

"And *we* are distractions?"

"Yes. White people are distractions."

James grabbed a bunch of stringy bark and threw it into the fire. He watched the fibres curl up and turn white before vaporizing in a flash of orange.

"Well how long will it take his people to finish these preparations, this praying, whatever?"

Pam asked Billy the question. "He doesn't know."

"Well, could he make a rough estimate?"

"But you don't seem to understand, James—this isn't a transitory event. It's not some *situation* that will resolve itself in a few days."

"I know. I know. These tribal land claims are a long term investment. Our government understands that, and we're prepared to negotiate. Tell him that, Pam. Please, tell him."

Pam shrugged and delivered the irrelevant message.

"Well?" James asked.

"There is nothing to negotiate—that's what he says."

"Look, Billy—you tell him this, Pam—there's no point in being hard-nosed. The government recognizes that there are legitimate aboriginal land claims, but any claim must be based on a realistic assessment of what the government can offer. There has to be give and take on both sides."

Again James could see Billy's irritating smile. What was so funny?

"Billy says the land is not for you to give. It is already his because he lives here and cares for it. He wonders how White People can separate the land from the people. Don't they understand that they're the same thing? He asks if you understand the White Man's thinking?"

James was finding it harder and harder to meet the elder's gaze; instead he stared at the ground. "No, no, I don't understand it, not entirely. All the same, what was the purpose of the walkabout? Ask him, Pam. Why did he want to take me on a walkabout? I don't understand."

"It's not important," answered Billy, "that you understand, only that you remember."

"Christ, Pam!" James yelled, "Did you know he spoke English?"

Then Billy pointed with his stick to that same patch of sky that James had been glancing at earlier. It was so lovely, so alluring. Billy waved James and Pam over and had them sit beside him. He pointed again and, as they followed the length of his stick, they noticed a thin finger of rock in the distance. If James wasn't mistaken, it seemed to be pointing back to Uluru and then, up from Uluru, ten degrees above the horizon, was a star, one of many in that rich section of sky. It wasn't too far from the Southern Cross.

"He's pointing to some star, isn't he? Which one?"

It was actually quite bright and, although James didn't know his sky particularly well, he had the feeling that this was a star he'd never seen before. "Is there something significant about this star?" James asked.

Billy stared deeply into his apprentice's eyes and smiled.

CHAPTER FOURTEEN

The old man stopped and signalled the others to lie down on their backs. Directly above them hung Djulpan, the Canoe, and the three brothers busy with their visitors from across the waters, bleached men from faraway lands, men without hearts.

But, look; there was something new: a second Purra off to the left amid the star cloud they call The Pit. It was not one of the Wanderers because the Wanderers had to always keep to the road. Still, there it was... shining brighter than Purra or even the bow and stern lights of the canoe. Only Sirius surpassed it in brilliance.

"It is Home Star," the Old Man explained.

They looked steadily eastward as the wind blew wildly through their hair. Behind them, Home Star cast long shadows far back across the bumpy monolith. They watched for hours, till Djulpan had drifted many hand-widths across the sky. What could it mean?

When they arrived back at camp, they made a fire and the aroma of burnt gum filled the air, quieting, for a moment, the canine madness surrounding them. The stars sank slowly in the West, Home Star reluctant to join them. Already, the eastern sky was paling, and the pit-fire glowed a deep and dying red.

"Do not be anxious," said the Old Man, as he poked a stick into the fire, "this is not the final brightening."

For an instant, James couldn't remember where he was—only that he'd had another of those disturbingly vivid dreams. Why was it so cold? And what was the dream about? God, it was so cold! Only a few glowing embers remained in the fire, but Pam's arms and legs were draped all around him, so how bad could it be?

And then James almost jumped out of his skin— was proud of himself for not doing so—when he noticed opposite him, curled up beside Billy, a full-sized dingo. A wild dog! My God! It lifted its head to look at James, then, deciding all was well, went back to sleep. I'd just better … not … move, James decided. *I'll stay perfectly still.* Which he might have done, if at this very moment, he had not been overcome by a bout of hiccuping.

"James?" Pam asked sleepily, "Can you put some more wood on the fire?"

"It's all right, Pam. I'll just hold you—like this." He hiccuped again. "There, that's better now, isn't it? Now go back to sleep." As James patted Pam on the back, he turned his head very slowly to the west. At a pace that wouldn't attract the attention of dingoes, trying with all his might to stifle yet another rising hiccough.

There it was: Home Star, only brighter than it had been even a few hours before. *That* must be Eta Carinae. That must be the star he asked the Minister to check up on. But what the devil did Billy mean by the Final Brightening? Wait a second—did Billy even say that?

If only my uncle were here, James thought. He knew the answer to everything his five-year old nephew had ever asked him. He even predicted that one day James would grow up to be a *very important man, a big shot, a world class cricketer! Maybe even Prime Minister!*

CHAPTER FIFTEEN

"Yes, Prime Minister."

In spite of the cackling of a nearby kookaburra, the Minister had succeeded in transforming the quality of his voice to something rather staid, more awash with parliamentary competence.

"Yes, that's right, Prime Minister. I was the one who made the phone call."

Patrick Mahoney gently pushed away the adoring hand of the young Melbourner who clung to his elbow. "Not now, Crystal." Crystal pouted, retreated to her lounge chair, making sure as she did, that her robe would not obscure her magnificent God-given (one fantasized) cleavage.

"Well, I thought there might be, yes." The Minister covered his naked ear, found it necessary to walk away a few steps beyond Crystal's reach. "You don't say? Well, yes, that's quite amazing, isn't it? Thank you, sir. And you say the science boys are pretty happy? Well, that's good. Yes ..."

A tiny bead of sweat began to accumulate at the top of the Minister's temple.

"Of course, Prime Minister. I have my best man there now." The bead reached full proportion and began sliding down Patrick's cheek.

"Yes, sir. Well, if you think that's best, sir."

Another bead followed. His entire body began to perspire. This is the way it used to be in interviews with his high school teachers. He thought he'd finished with all that.

"Yes, I think there's a flight this afternoon. I will, sir. I should be in Alice by morning.

"Of course, sir. I understand. Good-bye."

Patrick Mahoney, the Minister for Parks and Aboriginal Affairs, paused and considered before he spoke. He stared intensely at the young Melbourner who sat in the lounge reading her paperback, knees pressed up provocatively against her breasts.

"Crystal? How would you like to take a trip to the Rock?"

Crystal sat up, removed her sunglasses: "What?"

"Ayer's Rock. We'll eat lunch and then start packing."

CHAPTER SIXTEEN

The two men walked outside in the morning sun. The temperature was perfect, but within an hour, it would be too hot.

Felix looked at Frank. "It's a real bummer, mate."

"It's not unexpected," Frank replied.

Despite Greg's assurances, Frank had been pushed off the project. They were quite willing to have him there as a physical presence, but that was all. All the research decisions were going to be made by Cooper and Hollis.

"You know," said Felix, "I'm between projects at the moment, and now it seems as if you are too. Why don't we do something out of the ordinary with our free time?"

Felix was irrepressible. You couldn't help but smile.

"What do you have in mind?"

"Oh, I don't know ..." Felix kicked a stone. "Did Maggie tell you her story?"

"What story?"

"About the aboriginal elder who predicted the supernova."

Frank's eyes widened.

"She didn't tell you?"

Felix re-told the story, embellishing it freely. "So what do you think?" Should we investigate? You can be Inspector Poirot and I'll be Miss Marple!" Felix's cackling laugh followed, causing a flock of cockatoos to veer in their flight and check out this unusual sound. Just a crazy human. They continued on their way.

Frank stopped walking. "You want to go to Ayer's Rock?"

"Yes. Why not?"

"Just like that?"

Felix snapped his fingers. "Just like that!"

"But they're not even flying in there right now. They've closed down the airport."

"Oh, it's no problem, my friend. I have arranged us a charter. The pilot thinks I'm aboriginal."

"Felix?" Frank's eyes narrowed.

"Yes?"

"*What* exactly would we be investigating?"

"Well I think we should speak to that aboriginal astronomer, don't you? If there's any truth to Maggie's story, he may well have something to teach us."

Frank could only shake his head.

"Well, perhaps he really *did* know when Eta Carinae was going to explode—it would be interesting to learn how he knew this, wouldn't you agree?"

"But *how* could he know?"

"Ah, well, that is the sixty-four thousand dollar question. But, we've heard of things just as strange in the past. That tribe in Africa which somehow knew that Sirius had a white dwarf star orbiting around it—how do we explain that?"

"But that's just folklore; it's not hard data."

"Well sometimes folklore is all we have to deal with. If we're going to be astro-historians, Frank, we must be open-minded. Maybe this chap—maybe his tribe—have recorded in their folklore a long history of brightenings by Eta Carina. Would that be of interest to a post-graduate astronomer?"

"Felix, the last thing I need right now is another bloody idea for a thesis!"

"Oh come on, Frank, don't be a dickhead. I know you're as anxious to go as I am."

Frank shook his head, smiling broadly. "Felix, where do you get this language?!"

"What? Is there something wrong with *dickhead*? I hear Greg use it all the time."

Frank laughed, picked up a stone, and threw it over the embankment outside the observatory grounds. "So where's this plane then?"

CHAPTER SEVENTEEN

The walk back to Uluru had seemed much shorter. James and Pam immediately went for a swim—James more of a waddle—and then went to their rooms to put on fresh clothes. Afterwards, they met to discuss dinner. They sat in lounge chairs staring with disbelief at the great slab of water which still sloshed gently against the sides of the pool.

James shook his head slowly. "God, just think of carbon footprint we're making."

Pam nodded.

The proprietor approached with his broom. He muttered lowly to himself, a bitter Sisyphus, bound forever to his task of sweeping.

"Are we the only ones here now?" James asked.

The proprietor, looked up, somehow keeping intact the immense length of ash which hung from his cigarette.

"The Germans left, but there's still those other two foreign blokes."

"The Finns?"

"Yeah, that's right. Funny name for people isn't it? Good name for sharks."

"I see your point."

Pam rolled her eyes.

James marched bravely on "Do you have anything to eat? I realize your stocks must be low."

"Roo."

Pam shrugged.

"You want I should slap a few slabs on the barbie?"

"Well," continued James, "that would be great, then. Kangaroo for two, please."

"You have to cook it yourselves."

"No worries."

The level of the swimming pool had dropped about two feet. It seemed like there were no plans to top it up. At this rate, the water should evaporate completely in about a week. James hoped to be long gone by then. He wondered about the Finns.
"We visited Ayer's Rock today!"

"How was it?"

"It was *awesome!*" The Finns were pleased with themselves for using vocabulary they thought *contemporary*.

"Very, very nice!" added the other Finn, "but the climbing—it was not permitted."

"No?"

"No one may climb now."

"Really"

"Ayer's Rock is ... " The two Finns consulted for the right word—one had dictionary in his hand. "It is *sacred*. Only for aboriginals."

"It's been that way for a while, mate."

The Finns again spoke to each other in their native tongue.

"*You* are aboriginal, yes?"

"Yes," James replied cautiously, "I am."

"Jaan wants to take video of you. Okay?"

James looked over at Pam who was almost bursting to avoid laughing.

"Okay. What do you want me to do?"

"Do nothing. Just be natural. Good. Like that."

James stared into the camera, mesmerized by the infra-red focuser and then, seized by a sudden inspiration, crossed his eyes and wagged his tongue like a Maori warrior.

"Thank you," Jaan said. "Thank you very much!"

Then the Finns left and it was quiet again.

All James and Pam wanted to do was stare up into a sky which was the very definition of blue and serenity. What more could anyone ever want than this? To be here, in a lounge chair, staring up at the vast blue Australian sky.

Over the past forty-eight hours, James had become re-accustomed to the quiet of the land, remembered how he loved it and needed it. He was quite shocked when a plane roared overhead.

"Good God! What's that?"

"It's just a plane, James. Relax."

"Well, where's it going to land? The airport's closed."

"It's a small plane. It can land anywhere." The plane circled once around the airport. The runway was spotted with boulders and unusable, so it banked back towards the hostel. It seemed to have found a landing place and began to drop in altitude, heading for a spot perhaps a kilometre away. "I wonder who's in it?"

James laughed. "Probably my boss!"

The noise of the plane almost, but not quite, drowned out the noise of the bus from Alice Springs which was just then coming to a stop in front of the hostel. There were only two passengers on board, one of whom James immediately recognized.

"Here we are now," said the Minister. "Be a good sheila, don't block the doorway."

CHAPTER EIGHTEEN

The plane finally came to a halt just before a three-metre-high sand dune. Within half a minute the engine was off and the propellers still.

Frank had been squeezed tight behind the two front seats, but finally made his way loose. "That's got to be the bumpiest landing I've ever experienced." With immense relief, Frank jumped out the confines of the three-seater Cessna. It was good to be on the ground again, any ground.

"It was exciting, I'll give you that!" Felix inhaled the air. He seemed positively energized by the landscape, the setting sun, Uluru, and the great red desert which encompassed him.

"Come on then, chaps!" Felix waved to Frank and the pilot. He had stuffed a hankie into the back of his cap and fantasized that he was in the French Foreign Legion. "This way!" Felix yelled, and his companions dutifully began tramping through the sand with him, heading towards the vacant hotels, perhaps the Lost City of the Kalahari.

They hadn't gone far before Frank stopped. "Look! "Look behind you! It's not dark yet and you can already see it. Must be zero magnitude at least!"

"Holy smokes!" Felix replied, "it's not supposed to do that!"

CHAPTER NINETEEN

"Jimmy boy!" There was a pause as the Minister eyed Pam thoroughly and tried to decide if she was really with his assistant. Didn't seem likely.

"Well, Jimmy boy, just thought I'd drop in and check on how things are going." The Minister then patted James on the back, even winked at him. "How *are* you going, Jimmy?"

"Fine, Minister."

"Good. Glad to hear it." The Minister took James aside, almost stepping on a gecko as he went. "And about that little *problem* we've been having with access to park?"

"Well, sir," James replied, "I haven't quite got the details worked out *yet,* but I've got another meeting scheduled with the elders tomorrow morning."

"Oh well, that's good then. At least you've got the ball rolling."

"Thank you, sir."

"Oh, pardon my manners." The Minister motioned to his companion, "I'd like you to meet, Crystal—my personal secretary. Crystal's from Melbourne, James, your neck of the woods."

My God! It *was* her! James had gone to school with her. But she didn't have any breasts in tenth year. James stared at her wide-eyed. She returned his stare.

"G'day," Crystal said, extending her hand. "A pleasure."

That voice. He'd never forget that voice. "G'day," James returned. "I have the feeling perhaps we've met before. I think maybe —"

"Nah, nah, I don't think so. I would have remembered."

"Oh, well, maybe not." She very definitely had breasts now. "It's been a long while since I've been in Melbourne."

"Yeah," Crystal replied, "is there a toilet close by?"

Pam pointed the way. James half-expected her to go with Crystal, but she didn't.

"Well," said the Minister, "something smells good!"
Felix's group, drawn by the same aroma, entered the patio a moment later. Felix marched forward confidently.

"Greetings, my friends. I hope you are all well. We are looking for an aboriginal person by the name of Billy."

approaching the base of Uluru

CHAPTER TWENTY

It was an unlikely troupe which set out for the face of Uluru at dawn the next morning. Billy led the way, behind him the two women, then the astronomers and finally, James and Patrick. The pilot begged to stay home, claiming the kangaroo had disagreed with him and was bounding about in his stomach.

"I can't believe I'm doing this," Crystal confided to Pam. "I can't believe I'm out in the middle of nowhere on some aboriginal bush walk." Pam smiled. "God! My hair's just one big tangle! Ow!" In the middle of her tirade, Crystal had brushed up against some spinifex. "Jesus! I'm bleeding!"

Felix rushed up to have a look at the wound. "It's just a scratch," he announced. "You'll be right as rain."

"I hope so," Crystal replied, pouting as if she were in a Miss Melbourne beauty pageant which, indeed, she had once been.

"Oh, there's no doubt about it, madam. No cause for alarm."

James had become keenly aware how out-of-place human speech seemed in this place.

"I don't know why the hell Mr. Billy here can't negotiate over a table like the rest of the civilized word. Did you try to get him to come to a table?"

"I did, sir. But he insisted on coming here."

"Bloody hell. We'll be frying like omelettes in a couple of hours."

"We should be at Uluru by then. It's nice there. We can sit in the shade."

James was amused to the find that the bush flies had specially picked out the Minister to bother. They whirled round his head in attack formation.

"God-damn flies! Why don't they bother *you?*"

"They do sometimes, Minister. I think the trick is to stay calm."

"Calm?! You expect me to be bloody calm when the little buggers are flying up my nostrils!"

"They can sense your excitement. That's what Billy says."

"So, Billy's a bloody expert on bush flies too, eh? Wish we could nuke the whole damn lot of them!"

The walk continued in a similar vein, except that, after awhile, the newcomers were too exhausted to talk. Felix was an exception. He enjoyed the heat and said the countryside reminded him of home.

By 10:30 they had reached the foot of Uluru. It was even more impressive than James had imagined. There were nooks and caves and cavities everywhere, a tremendous complexity of textures. Plants of all kinds—tall trees in some cases—had taken root in the shelter of the great monolith. It was an oasis in the desert, a little Eden. It was only fifteen minutes along the circumference before they came to a little water hole. It was pristine and clear. It was here that Billy made camp.

"So, now we can finally talk," the Minister managed to say in a gasp, as he collapsed to the ground.

"No," James replied, "first we rest."

"What!" It was automatic. Patrick had to protest against any idea which didn't originate with him. He could only manage short sentences. "Well, all right then ... For half an hour ... Then we'll talk." Crystal collapsed on the ground beside him. Within seconds, both were asleep.

Frank followed the elder's example and leaned back against a white gum. He wasn't sleepy but he felt the need to close his eyes, to let his mind wander, to let all the tension and connection with outside world slip away as it so desperately needed to.

Felix too welcomed the peace. He took a book from his knapsack and began to read about a far distant time, about a time when gods and men shared the same forests. Time was cyclical, his Hindu brothers argued. In a place like this, Felix said to himself, it just seemed possible. Felix bit into an apple. He must give it some more thought.

Finally all human sounds subsided. That was good. This was a holy place.

James thought he would explore for a bit. Where was Pam? She had been here just a minute before.

James followed the waterhole as it curved around the steep cliff-face. As he turned the corner, he heard singing. My God! It was beautiful. But what was she singing? It wasn't English? What was it? And *where* was she?

Finally, after reaching a clump of emu brush, James spotted Pam—she was washing her hair, her hands holding the wet strands above her shoulders and her bare back gleaming in the sun. The small ripples in the pond reflected off her skin. She continued to sing, the modulations of her voice like butterflies flitting among the blossoms. James had never seen or heard anything so sweet and could not understand how he did not collapse on the spot in outright ecstasy.

> *Murgah Muggui appears to men as a beautiful young woman. Often she is found at waterholes where she entices men with her hypnotic singing. She does all in her power to persuade young hunters to lie with her. "Just rest a little while," she says. "You must be tired. Let me massage your weary limbs and you will feel better."*
>
> *But Murgah Muggui is not a real woman. She is a spider, and once she has put her victims to sleep, she kills them with a sharpened yam stick. In the morning, all that is left of them is an empty shell.*

Pam turned around. Her bare breasts exploded like bombshells in James's heart.

"James? Is that you?"

James wasn't sure if was him or not.

"You wouldn't happen to have a comb, would you?"

Without ever knowing how he managed to retrieve comb from pocket, transfer comb to hand and hand to Pam, James watched in helpless reverie as she stroked again and again her beautiful long hair. *Murgah Muggui.* He hadn't realized her hair was so long. Finally finished, Pam turned and smiled.

"What was that you were singing?" James asked.

"An old Celtic love song. Did you like it?"

"Yeah". He could hardly speak.

"Here's your comb back."

"No, no, I want you to keep it."

Pam laughed. James didn't know why. He didn't care.

"James?" Pam motioned to him. "Come and sit over here; you must be tired."

Was this Dreamtime? Was it real? Was there a difference? Still, somehow, James found himself moving, floating, Pam's smile growing ever larger. He knew only the red beneath and the blue above, and dimly, somewhere in the most distant recesses of his understanding, James sensed a flapping of wings, wings coming closer. It was his *mood-jin-garl*—the magpie who, for half of eternity, watched the two of them intently from a neighbouring gum tree.

CHAPTER TWENTY-ONE

When James and Pam arrived back at camp, they found Felix and Billy heatedly exchanging gestures and drawing in the sand. Felix had already learned dozens of aboriginal words and seemed confident, given enough time, he could decipher all of Billy's story.

"You want some help?" Pam asked.

"You speak Pitjantajara?"

"Yes."

"Marvellous! You know it's quite amazing, this man's knowledge of the sky. We've been drawing star maps in the sand and he's been showing me the locations of several supernovae, one in Lupus of which, up until now, we've had no recorded sightings of whatsoever. But the details—well, there's only so much you can draw in the sand."

"What would you like me to ask him?"

Felix scratched his head. "Where does one start? Ask him, please, if his people remember the last time Eta Carinae brightened?"

Frank had now awoken and walked over to join the discussion. James quietly slipped away and examined the nearby emu brush. It had delicate little white flowers, with a bit of pink in the middle. You could extract poison from the blossoms and use it to poison waterholes. But it was only poisonous to emus. Remarkable.

"And before then?" Felix continued, "did Eta Carinae brighten before then?"

"Only once," Billy explained, "in the dreamtime, when Uluru was first formed."

"Well that hardly seems likely," Frank mused. "Geologically,

Uluru's a couple of hundred million years old, far older than Eta Carinae."

"Perhaps ..." Felix could not take his eyes off the old man. "And this brightening now, how bright will it become? As bright as Venus?"

There was a little confusion about this question, but Pam finally seemed to get it right. She translated "morning star" for Venus.

"Brighter," Billy says."

"How much brighter?" Felix intended to pursue this question to the end.

Frank shook his head, poked a stick at the star maps in the sand. "How could he possibly know, Felix?" With one swoop, he wiped out Lupus. "Or should I call you *Miss Marple*?"

Felix laughed. "Miss Marple is well-bred enough not to contradict her elders!"

Pam pointed upwards toward the crescent moon, north-west of them. "Billy says it will become as bright as Deet."

"Deet? The moon?"

"Yes."

"That bright?!"

Frank could no longer sit. "But it *can't*, Felix. It's not close enough. Betelgeuse, maybe—but Eta—it would have to be some entirely new class of supernova. He's just making a wild guess." Frank was playing the sceptic. He had to. Felix wouldn't.

CHAPTER TWENTY-TWO

The Minister was peeved. He couldn't understand why Billy was being so obstinate. Didn't he understand that he was the Minister? That he had power to give land or take it away? Couldn't he understand that his people's entire future depended on making reasonable—the Minister made Pam emphasize the word—reasonable accommodations with Canberra?

"There's no two ways about it, mate," the Minister explained, "this park is going to be re-opened, one way or another." Even from Patrick's particularly narrow vantage point, he could perceive that threats made no impression on Billy.

"Well, look then, Billy—" perhaps he would respond to pleading —"if you would just give me a *reason*, a timeline and a reason— I might be able to sell *that* to the Prime Minister. Say, you were holding religious functions or something—and the ceremonies would be over in a week—and then everything returned to the status quo—we might be able to live with something like that."

It seemed to be Pam's translation of the word "status-quo" that amused Billy so. He had to cover up his mouth to stop from laughing.

"What the hell does he find so funny?" the Minister asked.

"I'm not sure," Pam replied, although she too had to cover her mouth. It was contagious. James was smiling too. So too were Felix and Frank.

"What the hell is so funny? What's the matter with you people? Is it some great lark to be out here in the middle of nowhere negotiating with goannas and bush flies! Is this your idea of a good time! I would have thought you were as anxious to be finished with this business as I am! Christ!"

The Minister turned to James who, chameleon-like, had made his face appear serious. "I thought you said we were going to meet *elders*—in the plural? Where are the rest of them?"

"They're coming, sir. At dusk, I think."

"At dusk! How long is it before dusk?"

Frank looked at his watch. "Another couple of hours, Mr. Mahoney." He was as anxious as the Minister. He was waiting to see how bright Eta Carinae would become.

CHAPTER TWENTY-THREE

The Minister was livid. It was dusk and, as promised, a dozen of half-naked black elders appeared, seemingly out of nowhere. But no one would talk to him. The elders talked among themselves, and seemed to point to James and even to Felix from time to time. The Minister, however, was totally ignored.

"James?" Pam asked, smiling. "Ready for another walkabout?"

James nodded. He took a quick sip from his water bottle then lifted his pack to his shoulders. "You know, Pam, this all seems quite familiar somehow."

"That's a good sign."

There was something odd about the look in Pam's eyes. "*You*'re coming, aren't you?"

Pam shook her head. "I haven't been invited."

Billy was waving to James. The elders were anxious to go and murmured a faint chant as they rose to their feet.

Pam kissed James on the cheek, lingered longer than she had meant to, then moved quickly over to Felix. "Up you go, Doctor. Your journey's only just begun."

Felix had been daydreaming, watching a beetle crawl through the sand. "What?"

"They're inviting you for the walkabout."

"Really?" Felix laughed. "Well, I accept. Without hesitation!" Quickly, Felix grabbed his pack and he and James melted into the crowd of dark bodies.

"Hey! Just a minute," exclaimed the Minister, "where do you think you bunch are going?" But no one paid attention. Already the line of men had begun their march westwards. The Minister tapped Crystal on the arm then pointed towards the motley trekkers. "Cripes, there's a sight you don't see everyday."

From a distance, James could just hear the Minister's postscript. "And don't forget, it has to be a *reasonable* accommodation!"

climbing Uluru

The elder at the front of the line was unusually lithe, and one sensed he was accustomed to being the leader of walkabouts. He led them in a very quick pace. The sun had set and it was rapidly growing dark, but they moved as if the dark would be no impediment.

Soon it was the noises of cicadas which filled their ears, growing louder as the darkness descended, as if each insect had attached itself to a brightening star.

Suddenly the details of his walkabout dream came rushing back to James. He was climbing Uluru. He and a band of young men and elders—together they were climbing Uluru in the darkness. "Felix," he yelled out in excitement, "I've done this before!"

"I can tell, my friend."

The path started steeply. For the benefit of tourists, it had long ago been outfitted with metal posts linked by chains. The posts were polished from constant use. You could see the reflection of the moon in them.

James was grateful for the handholds. He looked behind to see if Felix was still there. He was, and he was smiling.

"Quite the walkabout!" This was all Felix cared to say or could say. He too preferred to focus on the metal chain before him rather than plunging to his death.

Below Felix, and past the two or three elders behind, it was almost totally black. Two or three lights came from the hotel area, and someone seemed to have started a fire near the base of the monolith. Except for this, it was all stars. Stars which surrounded them, bathed them, danced off the surface of waterholes. Their combined light seemed almost capable of providing warmth.

Even in the light of the rising moon, Warrambool (the Milky Way) could be easily seen stretching from the north over the great arm of Orion, down by the Great Dog into the sail of Vela and then —this was something new....

CHAPTER TWENTY-FOUR

Frank rose from the campfire. He knew if he moved just a little to the north, he should be able to see Eta.

"Where are you going?" the Minister asked. He held Crystal in his arms, making the best of a bad situation.

"Need to take a leak," Frank answered.

"Watch out the dingoes don't get ya!" The Minister laughed and Crystal with him.

Frank smiled until he was out of view behind the rock face. With only an endless wilderness now before him, Frank began to speak to himself out loud—a charm against ghosts. "Shouldn't be much farther. Watch the bloody spinifex, Frankie boy. Yes, there's Puppis. Just a little further." Then he stopped. "My God! There it is! My God, Felix, can you see!"

CHAPTER TWENTY-FIVE

The trail levelled out. They were now atop the monolith, and suddenly a great blazing star appeared in the sky. No other star could rival it. Not Sirius, not Canopus. James looked behind him and saw his shadow twice, once cast by the moon and once by this new star.

"My God!" Felix exclaimed. But his voice was no more than a squeaky whisper. The scene completely overwhelmed him. "Then it's true! Holy smokes!"

Everyone sat down. A chanting had begun and James heard sticks beating together. One man rose up and began to dance. His movements were impossibly athletic, almost comic, and for a moment James thought he recognized the dancer as Billy. But these were the movements of a young man whose athletic silhouette could be seen against the rich knots of Milky Way in the south, and particularly against the white brilliance of Eta Carinae —Home Star. Sky Dancer danced like the kangaroo, he danced like the emu, he danced like the cockatoo and seemed ready to jump into the sky and stay there. And finally, as his finale, he danced as the goanna and James realized, after all, that it *was* Billy.

The dancing stopped, then the beating of the sticks—but the chanting continued.

"Why do they call it Home Star?" Felix asked.

"I'm not sure. Somehow they associate it with their ancestors. Billy told me Home Star was created at the same moment as the People. And when it reappears like this, somehow it is supposed to take them home again. I didn't really understand what he was getting at."

They both watched in silence for several minutes as Home Star blazed above them. A warm wind blew into their faces.

"You know, my friend, this could be the end for us."

"I know," James replied, although he wasn't sure *how* he knew. He wasn't even quite sure what a supernova was.

"We are witnessing," Felix continued, "the biggest light show in the galaxy and for sure, it has meant the end of any civilization in its vicinity. Terrible death. Terrible destruction."

"And yet it's so beautiful...."

"Yes ... And even now heavy elements like gold and silver and plutonium—they are streaming out of the star's centre to all the corners of the Milky Way, bound for the centres of new stars, new worlds—so, even in the throes of cataclysm, there is a kind of hope."

"A silver lining."

Felix laughed. "I suppose! And those same particles are streaming here toward Earth where we do not really need them—that's the problem, I'm afraid. It's a shame."

James thought of Pam, of his mom, all his cousins and his Uncle, even his secretary back in Canberra, all the people he had ever known in fact, and imagined them all stretched out in a straight line across the desert, all holding hands, all connected, all looking up.

"Of course," Felix continued, "what we don't know about Eta Carinae could fill books. Many shelves worth."

James turned and saw starlight glint off Felix's teeth. He wondered if he would ever have a chance to better know this strange and likeable man.

"It might not even be a supernova at all," Felix continued. "It certainly is not behaving like one—in fact, it is driving my colleague Frank Peterson quite out of his mind with its light curve!"

"I don't understand."

"That's the beauty of it, James. *We* don't understand either! It's what I most love about astronomy. All the things we don't understand!"

James laughed. "*That* I understand!"

"For all we know, Home Star could be a white-hole, or some white hole-worm hole combination." Felix extended his arm through the darkness and nudged James on the shoulder, "Raisins?""

"Thanks."

James accepted the gift with a gratitude far bigger than the occasion seemed to warrant. Both men chewed and pondered.

"A white hole, you think?"

"A theoretical object, mind you, but so once were electrons, and neutrinos, even cell phones."

"I've heard of *black* holes."

"Well, white holes would be their opposite, a place in the universe, where matter is not being sucked in but spewed out. Perhaps even a gateway to a parallel universe."

"A gateway?"

"Though how one would enter the gateway and avoid being blasted or crushed to smithereens —that is the sixty-four thousand dollar question. You'd have to speak to Kip Thorne." Felix could sense his companion's confusion. "Astrophysicist extraordinaire—expert on black holes, white holes, worm holes, a whole host of holes." Felix laughed, and his laughter seemed to make the stars twinkle. "Actually, with his propensity for describing breaks in the space-time continuum, I think he should be called Rip *Torn*! What do you think? More raisins?"

"Thanks." James felt as if he and Felix were engulfed in an immense spherical sigh. "So you were saying, you think there might actually be other universes?"

"Why not, my friend? Quite possibly an infinite number, countless numbers of which would be inhabited by a dozen dark men gazing skyward from the summit of a red monolith."

"Us, you mean?"

"Very like us, yes—perhaps indistinguishable."

"So, if there are an infinite number of universes out there, there could also be a particular universe that is identical to this one in every way except in a few particular details."

"Correct."

"There could be one in which Eta Carina is *not* exploding."

"A most desirable one to be in at this time."

"And one in which there is an Earth, an Australia, an Uluru, rugby, and all the things we love, except for a particular person named James Cook?"

"With infinity as your guide, my friend, you can custom-make your universe."

James could hear the astronomer swallow, then his lips curl into a smile.

"Just finished the last raisin, I'm afraid."

The wind seemed to blow from two directions at once. How could that be? But it was a nice, warm wind and it made James remember....

Only one night before, when Billy told his stories. It very late and James had to fight to keep himself from nodding off. But now he remembered in striking detail.

Byamee, the Sky King, made two men and one woman. He showed them which plants to eat, and then he left to go walkabout. All went well for the three humans until a great drought came to the land. The woman and one of the men learned to eat the kangaroo rat, so they kept well, but the other refused. He would not eat his fellow creatures. He grew hungrier and hungrier. Seeing no way out of his dilemma, he got up one morning and began walking in the direction of the sunset. The man and woman chased after him. After many days they found him. He was very weak from not eating. All he could do was sit in the shade beneath a white gum tree. They went up to him, hoping to take him back home when suddenly a large black devil with two fiery eyes raised the man up and dropped him into the centre of the tree. "What shall we do now?" the man and woman asked. But it was too late. The devil caused the sky to shake and the entire tree was raised into the sky and carried away to the stars, next to Warrambool. Two yellow-crested

*cockatoos (the Mouyi) chased after it. The man and the woman
stared up in disbelief at the tree which had been snatched into
the sky. Gradually, the tree faded away and all that was left
were four gleaming eyes: the eyes of Yowee, the Spirit of Death,
and the eyes of their friend, the first man to die.*
*To this day, one can see those eyes staring at us from the sky, and
also the cockatoos who are looking for a place to roost.*

At this point in the story, James must have nodded off, for James
remembered Billy throwing sand at him.

"What? I'm awake! What is it?"

After a moment, Billy continued:

*And that is how Death came into the world. It made the swamp
oaks sigh and the blood gums shed red tears. But our pain will
not be forever. One day, Byamee will return from his walkabout.
He will light a bright fire, and the bright fire will lead the man
from the darkness down a lit path. That day will come soon. And
the man shall come home.*

"Home star, they're calling it...."

"It is beautiful to behold, is it not?"

"Yes," said James, with certainty of judgement he had rarely
known.

As never before, the sky seemed brilliant with stars and
trails and stories. James knew that to look upward was to look
homeward. It was to see Sky Mother. It was to be warmed,
comforted, bathed by her stellar caress. James knew, in a way
that was beyond words, that he and all his loved ones were going
home. A new home, but much like the old home. Only better.
That's where they were going. Yes. And as far as James was
concerned, there would be room for whomever wanted to join
them. And it was all going to happen very, very soon.

"Well," said Felix, seeing all the others rising, "I guess it's time to
push off."

James put his arm around his dark-skinned cousin.

Felix smiled back at him. "You know, James, I feel a little bit like Moses coming down the mountain!"

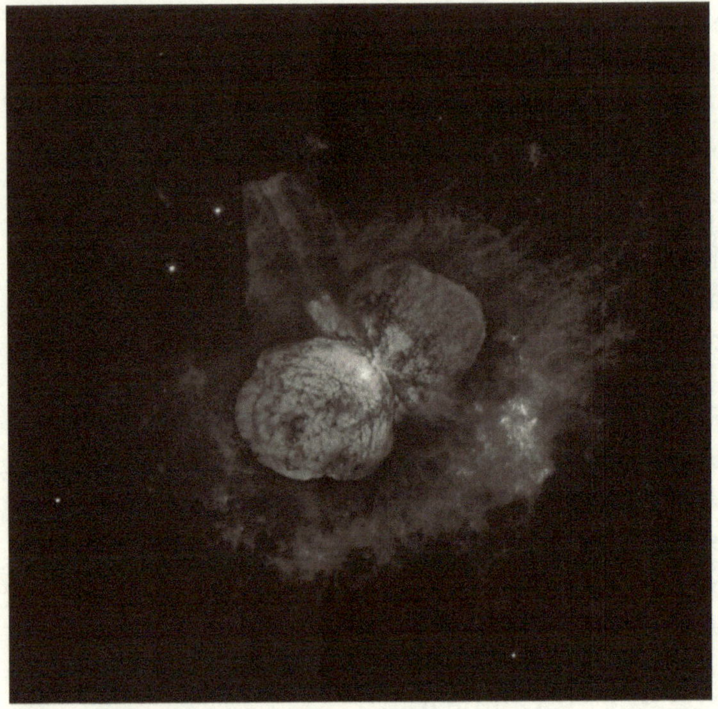

Eta Carinae—Image Credit: *NASA, STScI, and ESA*